HESPER'S WIZARD

DANTE KUN

Contents

1

Proud Nyber

A young wizard Nyber Khan
Looks down from his lofty perch
With loving self-protection
Upon an old forest of pine and birch.

On scarred battlements of black stone and light
Each night he's darkly stood
Wearing purple robes of ancient powers
And a gold embroidered hood.

He wears a Runic Bow of strong magic made
Mystic seeking arrows too
His dark blue sword of fine Elven steel
Shimmers straight and true.

A confusion spell of memory loss
He casts with great intent
The old forest will remain inviolate
On this his fierce will is bent.

He calls his new dragon "Hesper"
She's a tiny dragon too
Barely as large as an eagle
Her diamond scales shine a deep sky blue.

"Patrol" Nyber smiles without a sound
Thus true dragon-link gets done
Now bold Nyber Khan and Hesper
Linked together see as one.

With the emerald Dragonsight of Hesper
Fierce Nyber surveys the land
Over swaying fields of poppies blood red
And a deep blue lake ringed in silver sand.

Over mossy, ancient fir trees
Whose gnarled roots house gentle Gnomes
Over a magic singing stream
Where fair Water Fairies keep secret homes.

All is well in the emerald forest land
Watchful Nyber's eyes shine glee
For no human has crossed the boundary land
As far as young, proud Nyber can see.

Nyber's griffin is named Calibus
His thick fur is black-flecked gold
Nyber summons forth his brave griffin
And mounts the saddle proud and bold.

On griffin-back he starts the hunt
And climbs high a burgundy sky
For at twilight time he soars dusky clouds
As Calibus sings his war cry.

"It's hunting time" he smiles within
And Hesper further extends the link
Fierce Dragonsight engulfs his mind
Faster than a brave wizard can blink.

Calibus flies like a gale on a moonlit sea
The blue dragon is faster than light
For they see humans approach the boundary lands
And young Nyber likes to fight.

Yet there is no fight tonight for Nyber
Wild Hesper takes all the blame
As three sloppy, wasteful, loggers
Lie engulfed within royal blue flame.

On enchanted elven steel tonight
No greedy human blood will run
So towards castle keep they wheel as one
And they race the setting sun.

Seven stout Bugbears stand tensely waiting
When fierce Calibus finally claws black stone
They've all heard the young wizard hunting
They're all relieved he's come back home.

He chose to fly without bodyguards again
Chose to hunt wild from a blood red sky
They take him to task for this careless sin
And remind him that even wizards can die.

These seven are Nyber's brave generals
Commanding all of his bold goblin troops
For blue armored goblins patrol these protected lands
Weaving tight, concentric, swift loops.

For nighttime is not the lightime
And all around fierce goblins abound
Eagerly hoping greedy humans
Will trespass dark forested ground.

There will be no logging nor any mining
No polluting lakes or damming rivers too
Diversity will seek its wondrous way
Protected by warriors in armor blue.

The sun will rise, the sun will set
An alabaster moon will fly its course
Invaders by dark ones are cruelly met
For a pure forest is true magic's source.

So if you ever go out on a walk about
To explore a distant land
Stay far away from wide fields of poppies blood red
Near a turquoise lake ringed in silver sand.

And if you ever come upon a gargoyled castle
Carved of ancient obsidian stone
You had better just spin yourself right quick around
And run yourself right home.

For Nyber secretly fears all humans
As does Hesper and brave Calibus too
It's not really because they're human
It's because of things they've seen humans do.

Humans show no respect for ancient trees
Rare flowers, ferns, nor ancient rock
They dam up all free rivers
Ancient fairy streams they block.

They try to chop down every tree
And dig up all the land
They crave every fish in every lake
And they soil the ocean's sand.

They turn ancient forests into tree farms
Their nets choke the rivers life
They are the sworn enemies of diversity
Human greed is the source of strife.

When humans are done the land is always
Unlike it ever was before
A lifeless land devoid of trees
No safe home for bear nor boar.

No more ancient songs will flow from a fairy stream
No bright fish swim a deep blue lake
It's just the way they are these human kind
They've only learned to grasp and take.

For humans are just a fledgling race
Not as ancient as dwarves and elves
Not yet wise enough to consider others
As important as themselves.

Nyber knows well enough the ways of old
He knows some Dragonspeak
One day the humans will all grow up
And the old ways they will seek.

They will hear the ancient music from the planets
And singing from all the stars
They'll feel the sacred energy from their Mother Earth
And learn the old tales of Mars.

They'll hear the tones within the tones
Of fiery sunset, sand, and sea
They will learn the old ways of water and fire
And know sacred life dwells in every tree.

They will love walking much more softly
Thus not disturbing gentle Gnomes
They will better learn to build their houses
And not wreck forest homes.

They will learn to see the Dragons
Speak to Bugbears, Dwarves, and Elves
They'll ride swift and free on wild griffin back
And really enjoy themselves.

Then all ancient forests will be finally free
And never need to be patrolled
Then new time will turn full circle
And cycle back to a time of old.

But for now the young wizard, Nyber Khan
Looks down from his lofty perch
With loving self-protection
On an ancient forest of pine and birch.

Upon ebon battlements of stone and light
Alone he darkly stands
Wearing robes of much older powers
He surveys his armored bands.

His dark blue sword of elven steel
Shimmers straight and true
A Runic Bow spans his broad, strong back
A quiver of seeking arrows too.

Hesper The Elven Princess

Hesper is a wild turquoise dragon
She loves to soar the deep blue sky
And Nyber Khan the brash young wizard
Just loves to watch her fly.

She has diamond scales beyond royal blue
She sprays a wicked blue-white flame
Hesper has taught Nyber some dragon-speak
So Nyber can speak her true name.

She is as fast as light and dragon links
With bold Nyber while in flight
Barely larger than a giant eagle
She's full scale in any fight.

Her almond eyes are the deepest scarlet
Her pupils catlike and forest green
Her Dragonsight penetrates any darkness
And thus sees things almost never seen.

She dearly loves to tease wild griffins
As she dive-bombs the goblin troops
Nyber's Troops who patrol the land
In swift, concentric, tough loops.

It's all just good, clean, dragon sport
Her team is never close to being harmed
The wild griffins and generals ignore her
But the goblins get a little alarmed.

Nyber smiles and Hesper just knows
Thus perfect dragon link gets done
Earthbound Nyber gets quite a ride
As sweet Hesper has her fun.

For he then sees all a dragon sees
As wild Hesper soars the sky
In colors he's never seen before
As forest and field fly by.

Hesper loves to link up at night
And this causes Nyber glee
For the dark time has its colors
Only fierce Dragonsight can see.

This brave wizard has learned much
But not quite enough just yet
For he's young and Elven foolish still
To think wild Hesper is just a pet.

Hesper has some secret plans for him
A quiet hope he doesn't yet know
His education is not quite finished
There are some new places he must go.

He must invade a dark oak wood
And therein seize a forbidden prize
There is a cruel wizard war before him now
Of twisted magic, fire, and lies.

For sweet Hesper is an elven princess
Cursed now to be a dragon is she.
Yet Nyber's true heart can save her
If only the truth he will see.

For centuries she's been cursed like this
Cursed of form and face.
Torn from her castle of rare purple stone
Her soft bed of saffron lace.

How Hesper had cried out to her people
Tried so hard to say just who she really was,
Yet elves do not speak as dragons speak
And evil is as evil does.

Her dear father knew her not,
Her loving mother was deceived just the same.
They could only see a strange dragon fierce
With turquoise scales and a royal blue flame.

The Elven kingdom turned upon her,
With cruel arrows, sword, and spear
Unknowingly attacking,
Their own Elven princess dear.

The dark, twisted one who did this,
Leered down from a craggy peak.
Sending forth his winged minions,
A rare blue dragon he now would seek.

A black dragon covets this fine Elven girl,
Of rare form and face so fair.
An ancient one, of great magic and force,
Will's princess Hesper to grace his lair.

The wicked changeling spell he sent forth,
Was most powerful and true.
It shaped shifted a sweet princess into a dragon,
With pretty scales of turquoise blue.

Yet a changeling spell can only work,
With what a person carries within.
He had not counted on her silver soul,
Nor a fine heart that held no sin.

He could never have known her new made form,
Would fly as swift as light.
He had no idea that her pure, strong heart,
Would never give up the fight.

On that cruel day Hesper lost her parents.
Her castle, lands, and people too.
How she has missed her rare purple castle,
And her soft bed of saffron hue.

She lost her world and all she loved,
On a cruel spring day long ago.
These are the secret things brave Nyber must hear,
Of the black dragon, brave Nyber must know.

For this brutal dragon's name is Bracken,
His cruel minions are many and bold.
He stalks sweet Hesper every night,
With dark magick from a time of old.

Yet Hesper has found some safety,
Within Nyber's protected, forested, glen.
She hopes this young wizard will be strong,
When great Bracken finds her again.

Young Nyber is an Elven prince,
Yet the ancient wizard way he's sought.
Now far from his unbending people,
Many new lessons he's been taught.

And Hesper can see Nyber's heart,
As all pure of heart can do.
Nyber's true heart is a heart of burnt gold,
And her heart is untamed sky blue.

She could not help but fall in love,
With one so warm and kind.
She hopes he will return her love,
When he completely knows her mind.

Yet love or not, she will run no more,
The time has come to stand and fight.
She has made some friends and allies strong,
She will face great Bracken's might.

She must win back her form, so she can be,
The fair princess she was born to be.
She must somehow defeat great Bracken,
And find a secret, guarded, oak tree.

Around which there is a silver cord,
And a wondrous silver jar.
From this trap she must free her true form,
If her brave wizard can fight that far.

Once the magick jar is cracked the wicked spell will be,
Not as it was before,
A blue dragon will fade, a princess will glow.
Just as young as she was, once more.

But for now a young wizard, Nyber Khan,
Looks out from a lonely perch,
As dappled sunlight glistens turquois scales,
Over an ancient forest of pine and birch.

He ponders a swift blue dragon,
Untamed, wild, and free.
He wonders aloud just how strange it is,
That a turquoise dragon had come to be.

He marvels at the old Elvish she speaks to him,
She seems to love his castle of ebon stone.
She teases and flirts with him every day,
He feels happy and no longer alone.

3

Great Bracken

His diamond scales gleam like an obsidian night,
His cruel eyes cast a blood red glow.
Volcanic flame and heat, white hot, blood red,
From his ebon fanged mouth he can blow.

He flies on six wings of bat leather black,
Gliding silent on the night time air.
He does as he wills, and then returns,
To his secret, underground lair.

Starlight is more light than Bracken needs,
He dearly loves to hunt in the dark.
He stalks patiently sweet Hesper, following all leads,
Where he's been, he's left a cruel mark.

Commanding his army of goblins and orcs,
On armored griffin they bravely fly.
Following an ancient river, twisting where it forks,
Stalking silent a blood red sky.

Curved swords all forged of mystic dragon steel,
Shimmering a wicked, deep purple hue.
Black spears and nets enchanted with spells,
Seeking sweet Hesper, pure and true.

A dark, dread force, cloaked in a black velvet night,
Ebon scales and obsidian armor reflect amber moonlight,
Mighty wings pump air, keeping straight on course,
Excitement becomes bloodlust within Bracken's cruel force.

They stalk an old river with a faint elvish glow,
Bracken's cold magick inside he lets gather and grow,
Flowing and growing to a place he's not been before,
Summoning a true vision of a place new in lore.

A place with wide fields of poppies bright red,
A deep blue lake kissing silvery sand.
A secret place patrolled by a bold wizards force,
A wondrous, protected land.

A pure and magic forest scented with pine and birch,
Maiden fern, red clover, granite rock.
On its fair border a powerful confusion spell,
Very few could ever hope to unlock.

The spell is an easy task for great Bracken,
For an earthbound mind Bracken's not.
A young, foolish wizard will soon rue the day,
That he ever tangled with Brackens dark lot.

For dark magick is Brackens pure majesty,
It took many hard years for him to know,
How to cast mighty spells, wield cold force,
In unstoppable ways, just so.

He smiles wide as sweet Hesper casts an innocent link,
Now close enough he learns the score.
He knows all her hopes and her innocent dreams,
About a young wizard, unknown before.

Hesper has not yet grown the power,
To sense her playful link was caught.
To understand cruel Bracken knows of everything,
She and her young wizard have thought.

Yet one thing remains outside his link,
Made from the darkest obsidian stone,
The young wizards castle, of ancient stone and light,
To great Bracken remains unknown.

This old castle was not built by Nyber,
The ancient powers built it long ago.
Within its impenetrable obsidian walls
Psychic links have no power to go.

Now Bracken smiles in darkened glee,
He's found the new place she chose to flee.
He'll invade the young wizards forest land,
And lay it waste with his nightmare band.

For no mere wizard can hope to stay the course,
Of mighty Bracken and his battle tough goblin force.
He will find this young wizard, hunt him down,
Grind him, break him, to the cold hard ground.

He will burn the forest, boil the blue lake,
Crush all those pretty poppies red.
He'll enjoy torturing the young wizards generals,
Those weak blue armored troops he'll shred.

But now a golden dawn approaches,
Bathing the earth in magenta soft light.
Bracken has learned the hard way over time,
To never squander or waste his dark might.

So he will sleep and avoid the day,
Awaiting patiently the darkness of night,
When once again safely cloaked in shadow
He will take up his silent and ruthless flight.

He's found sweet Hesper and he now knows the way,
He sleeps happy at dawn, and grins as he lay
In an emerald green cave, under a gnarled oak tree,
His dream time is now filled with how he hopes things will be.

4

Calibus the Brave Griffin

Calibus the fierce, brave griffin,
Sensed Bracken while in routine flight,
So he chose to go out on a scout about,
Amidst a chilly, blood moon night.

Much more brave than smart,
He flew swift a cloudless night sky.
For bold Griffins have no fear of death,
Nor concern for a cold, evil eye.

And how great Bracken smiled,
From his dark place deep within,
As he schemed, conjured, and lured,
That foolish, brave. Calibus in.

Thus bold Calibus did attempt,
What he felt should quick be done,
And Bracken grinned so wicked wide,
At an unfought battle now totally won.

Under a thick, forested canopy,
Bracken hid his black armored force,
Except two goblins riding griffin back,
Toward the warriors unwise course

In amber moonlight above cloud line,
They attacked Calibus throughout the night,
And brave Calibus gave them both,
A most magnificent and impressive fight.

Yet with each harsh victory hard won
He grew more wounded and torn,
And from under the thick forested canopy,
More new enemies were cruelly born.

After the first two attackers, came another five,
And those five griffin riders soon swelled to nine.
Calibus stopped counting at twenty,
For brave Calibus was fighting for time.

His tragic time had suddenly become timeless,
Held hostage to cruel war cries and blood,
Gripped now within gore on bloody claws,
Seized by Goblins, fresh-dead in black mud.

A timeless battle as dead griffins crash branches,
Plummeting silent to cold, hard, ground.
To lie within the ancient silence of all silence,
Within Death's cold absence of sound.

Many a black armored, griffin rider,
Calibus ripped clear of his vicious mount,
And screaming goblins plunged to unforgiving earth,
Far too numerous to count.

Yet Bracken calmly waited uncaring,
Let this skirmish take the whole night!
He smiles knowing brave Calibus will be his captive,
Before he feels the first morning light.

Brackens grim army is immense, he is wasteful and proud,
So he toys with brave Calibus above any cloud.
Calibus cannot advance and he cannot retreat,
Encircled by slashing enemies, he faces a bitter defeat.

As a griffin he's immune to Bracken's spell "dragon fright,"
For spells that cast fear cannot stop griffin-fight.
Yet Bracken has learned to work through the night,
For he knows well the benefit of avoiding the light.

Yet finally battle weary, clawed deep and torn,
Brave Calibus falls to cold earth and scorn.
Captured then, dragged, and chained to a rock,
He finally see's the wicked force he had no hope to block.

His true heart cries out to his dear wizard friend,
Against Bracken's vast army Nyber must bend.
How Bracken flames and roars in darkened glee,
Now Calibus is right where he wants him to be,

Bracken does not yet seek this wild griffins death,
He summons two griffin scouts, Halidor and Seth.
"Go to this foolish wizard, tell him thus:
He may, if he will, parley with us!"

With the ancient tradition thus followed,
Bracken rumbles sated deep within,
He will observe parley with this young wizard
An exchange only Bracken will win.

Brackens dark thoughts drift to sweet Hesper
Cold love and seething hate an equal mix,
And Bracken loves his final solution,
Her free will he knows how to "fix."

That ungrateful blue dragon Hesper,
Will soon be chained tight in a velvet cage,
Then Bracken's world will finally be ready
For the full measure of Bracken's dark rage.

So both Halidor and Seth flew the stygian night,
Allowing themselves to be captured while still in flight.
They eagerly crossed Nyber's charmed boundary land,
Letting his confusion spell place them well in hand.

They each stayed well focused deep within,
So great Bracken in link would soon know,
All about troop strength and forward defenses,
And a young wizard, Nyber Khan, Bracken's foe.

How Bracken grinned so very wicked,
At young Nyber's "cute" little confusion spell,
He released an ancient spell of counter,
So his armored troops might place themselves well.

A brave bugbear named General Crokus,
Entwined Halidor and Seth within his net.
He rubbed their burgundy-black griffin fur,
And counseled them not to fret.

For General Crokus respects all free griffins,
He knows they are fearless and fly any sky.
He knows they have no fear of death,
And they simply scorn the evil eye.

Upon towering battlements of black stone and light,
Crokus drops his netted prize.
Young Nyber Khan surveys them both,
With his wizened wizard eyes.

His over eager seeking spell
He cast much to quick right then,
For he was curious to learn both their names,
And all the places they have recently been.

Yet once he cast that seeking spell,
Into Bracken's subtle net he fell.
For seeking spells must always come back,
With crucial information that you may lack.

And there was fierce Bracken, as clear as day,
And within this cold vision he had much to say.
Their frozen link was now connected and Nyber took
A fearful look within Brackens secret book.

The dark magick within began to gather and grow,
Nyber saw many things he would rather not know.
He saw a boiled blue lake, soiled silver sand,
Crushed red poppies, and burned forest land.

His tough brave generals
Led well his blue armored troops,
They fought long, hard, and relentless,
From concentric, tight loops.

Yet each time their hopeless circle tightened,
They were forced to give up some land,
Countless blue armored warriors
Were cruelly cut from the band.

Bracken's battle mad troops,
Were numberless and bold,
His dark magick was timeless,
Malevolent and cold.

The blue fought courageous to the last,
To the end, until there were none.
They all died hard for freedom,
Lost in a vicious battle not won.

Then Nyber and dearest Hesper,
Alone within the cruelest night,
Would stand before the great horde,
And face Brackens unforgiving might.

In a flash of golden light,
Bracken's harsh vision was finally done,
Thus showing young Nyber,
He had nowhere to run.

True, he could fight the good fight,
Yet there was no way to win,
Nyber's ears were still ringing,
From the lost battle's great din.

So now comes the parley,
The old forms are strictly observed.
Bracken's black diamond claws,
Are most twisted and curved.

From his forefinger claw,
Black light is emitted,
"Your Calibus for sweet Hesper."
Thus fine parley submitted.

"One little blue dragon"
"To avoid all you've surveyed today."
"No need to lose any life,"
"Or your true wizard way,"

"No real need for this fight,"
"Your painful death or this war,"
"Just cage my blue dragon,"
"And you'll see Bracken no more."

Yet truly wise wizards always learn,
To seek balance and always find,
The many unlimited, unknown pathways,
Within the unexplored collective mind.

They know to trust their truest feelings,
And their inner promptings too.
They use the wizards high art of discernment,
In all they seek to do.

Though Brave Nyber sees no way he can win,
He still trusts his true promptings from deep within.
So he faces cruel Bracken deep in link,
His grey eyes find focus and do not blink.

Nyber sends forth his truth to power,
For he has decided to refuse to live unjust,
He answers brave, refusing to cower,
He chooses right action and a path of trust.

"Halidor and Seth I will give freely to you,"
"But I cannot help you enslave the free dragon blue."
"So please return brave Calibus home to me,"
"Forget this foolish war, just let us be."

"A free dragon can have no real quarrel with you,"
"She is just a playful, dragon blue."
"She has a divine right to her place in the sun,"
"From your tyranny I will refuse to run!"

"Fine Then!" Bracken rumbled earthquake deep,
"I'll crush all these weak forces you try to keep,"
"I'll love boiling your lake and soiling your sand,"
"I'll love torching your precious forest land."

"I'll shred all your fields of poppies bright red,"
"And I'll rip sweet Hesper from her secret bed."
"All under your command I will rip and tear,"
"Your weak blue armored troops will get you nowhere!"

"And when I've finally tired of torturing you,"
"I'll grind you up to make a stew,"
"A wizard stew of kith and kin,"
"And Nyber Khan will never be again!"

"A tasty meal I'll just love to eat,"
"Amidst your pretty blue armored troops in total defeat."
"I'll summon my crows to help consume you too,"
"And I will make her watch it all, your sweet dragon blue."

Nyber never even blinked,
Anyone sane might have thought he would.
Upon the ancient battlements of ebon stone and light,
Alone he darkly stood.

He wore his purple robes of magic power,
And his gold embroidered hood,
He stood tall and faced Great Bracken's vision
The only free wizard who could.

In a flash of emerald light Nyber broke the cold link,
Enough of this cruel Bracken for it was now time to think.
He motioned General Crokus quickly to his side,
"Mount your fastest griffin for there are places you must ride."

Nyber gave truthful counsel to all his generals,
He gave them all a choice,
He showed them Brackens cruel vision,
Yet they answered in one fine voice.

"We stay and fight" they all did say,
"We will make this Bracken rue the day,"
"That he brought war to us and our fair land,"
"This war will bleed his evil band."

"For we must cost him dearly here,"
"So other lands will never fear,"
"This dragon's deadly trespass upon their lands,"
"His wicked magick, his heartless hands."

And so these brave ones made ready for war,
To bring truth to a power with an evil core.
To give up their lives and homes and land,
And hopefully bleed this evil band.

They stand ready to sacrifice and bring a tough fight,
To keep from the darkness a small point of light.
To allow slavery for one allows slavery for all,
To fight for one person's freedom is to honor freedom for all.

As a dragon Hesper caught this evil, cold link,
Saw Brackens vision and her brave Nyber not blink.
Here pure heart was crushed when she saw his inner light,
To know full well she had caused this fight.

Her brave heart weakened for her handsome wizard was lost,
She will go back to cruel Bracken no matter her cost.
She so loved Nyber Khan for the strength of his heart,
But a war with wicked Bracken she now wanted no part.

Yet when she tried to cast link with great Bracken,
Her crafty wizard smiled deep within,
For Nyber has learned to catch well her links,
And thus learn where she has been.

Now Nyber cast the only spell,
Ever he cast against a friend.
And Hesper's silken dragon wings,
Just kept refusing to unbend.

"We stay and fight" she heard him sigh,
His wizard link well done.
"We fight him tough! We go down hard!"
"Thus evil has not won."

"How can we ever endure this?"
Hesper sobbed so hopeless and lost,
"This madness is all my fault"
"So I must bear the total cost."

Nyber just smiled and strengthened the link,
She heard and felt her wizard wink,
"One day at a time is what we do,"
"One day at a time is how we get through."

"We know the answer if we don't try,"
"We reach for new life and we don't die."
"To speak truth to power is often hard,"
"For the jester called life will deal the card,"

"So we must do what we know is right to do,"
"We form a wall with our brave warriors in armor blue."
"We make Bracken pay for all he gets,
"And we will never hedge our bets,"

"We make him pay across our board,"
"As we bleed his wicked, evil horde."
"One day at a time gets things done,"
"One day at a time gets tough battles won."

"You never chose the path he laid,"
"His cruel decision you never made,"
"So stay the course, give well your word,"
"And this spell I cast was never heard."

So sad Hesper gave her solemn word to stay,
And fight the good fight every day,
Her silken wings unfurled, and she gained flight.
She flew her very last patrol that night.

Bracken's forces were just a day's march away,
And there was so much more she wanted to say!
She loved this young wizard and she so cursed her form!
She longed with all her heart to be again elven norm.

But things not yet said, she could no longer say,
And now there would never be any way,
To become her true self, to just hold his warm hand,
To escape cruel Bracken and his hateful band.

So she took to wild flight,
A warrior still true.
Her emerald eyes flashed green fire,
Her diamond scales turquoise blue.

She vowed to fight hard,
And cost well Bracken's horde,
To make them all pay freedoms price,
Upon her doomed wizard's sword.

Hesper never chose this ugly way,
This dragon form, this fearful day.
She never chose to lose her only true home,
To be denied her freedom, be forced to roam.

Yet she has chosen a noble path,
For she has chosen truth to power,
Her brave wizard has done the sacred wizard math,
And there is no longer any need to cower.

She has seen the ancient wisdom within young Nyber,
When he refused Evil Bracken any cruel choice,
And she heard the ancient truth within all the brave generals,
As they spoke truth to power in one brave voice.

So she just watched her young wizard, Nyber Khan,
Studying ridgelines from his lofty perch,
Longingly last seeing,
His precious forest of pine and birch.

Upon ebon battlements of black stone and light,
Alone he darkly stands,
He raises a blue banner high in the wind,
And calls forth his troops to protect their lands.

His enchanted sword of elven steel,
Is shimmering a deep royal blue.
A runic bow spans his broad, strong back,
A quiver of seeking arrows too.

He sighs out loud with a sad smile within,
Another wizard link well done.
Young Nyber Khan and Hesper,
Hold a fierce link and see as one.

5

Flavious Pontificus Calendula, The Keeper of all sacred words

Flavius Pontificus Calendula,
Is The Keeper of all sacred word.
He receives and transmits all most patiently,
The mystic secrets only he first heard.

In a secret cavern underground,
Where silver fairy light does abound,
And nine emerald pillars circle round,
He fills an ancient book without a sound.

His diamond scales are white, crystal multihued,
Prism like, no light subdued,
Reflecting sun on polished abalone shell,
His pure crystal white shows all colors well.

Within Magenta fairy flame,
Ancient words appear,
Circling the emerald crystal columns,
For this sacred seer.

Within the circles center Flavious stands alone,
Imprinting the vision held in each crystal stone.
Midnight black is the color of his book,
Inside of which he does not look,

Bound in golden thread this ancient tome,
Becomes the flame words sacred home.
All dragon magic lies deep within,
For the Keepers job will never end.

Flavius scribes with pure mind, never a pen,
For he knows where all sacred words have been,
Within his golden cavern wild fairies dance,
As the Keeper keeps keeping, they spin and they prance.

All new wizard magic comes from here,
By passing through the walls of fear.
Daring dreams are pulled by Dragon trance,
And the ancient secrets within fairy-fire dance.

Magic within one must gather and grow,
And thus learn all the things a wise wizard should know.
Inside the unopened book there are ancient answers to see,
One just has to go where earthly mind cannot be.

Great Bracken has found it, from within yet without,
Awesome power he's grown as he's roamed about.
His nine darkest wizards have gone deep as well,
Yet even they will not go where he loves to dwell.

Flavious sighs deep as he reads the score,
He will have to act fast to balance up Bracken's war.
To unbalance the sacred scales is the only true sin,
Forcing The Keeper to fly where he's never been.

He must now find a young wizard,
And a blue dragon brave.
He must do battle with Great Bracken,
And the world he must save.

The ancient Tome of Mystery,
In Bracken's claws just cannot be.
For Bracken has no respect for living things,
Nor the gift of life warm sunlight brings.

Many things yet unseen Bracken then would know,
He would command volcanic winds to blow,
He could shake the earth, move every known sea,
And never again would the known world be.

After destruction Bracken would create anew,
Any kind of cruel world he wanted to.
His brand of darkness would replace all light,
Twisted bracken would rule with unbalanced might.

Great Bracken has knowledge of the unopened book,
For he's grown strong enough to sneak a look,
His focused mind can scribe without a pen,
For he's went farther than most have been.

Great Brackens crystal is a glossy black,
Within his secret space he's grown the knack,
Inside a purple flame dark words transmit,
And Great Bracken has a place they fit.

A great book with a cover of midnight blue,
All bound in cord a multi-hue.
In magick colors never seen in light,
Bracken binds his spells, preparing to fight.

Flavius sighs deep as he reads Brackens book,
In sacred link his emerald eyes never had to look,
For he is the Keeper of all sacred word,
Bracken's attempt at control is most absurd.

For the multiverse is not designed for control,
Discernment and Acceptance rule the day.
Cooperation and respect always grow a strong soul,
And fierce love is the only true way.

Some struggles you may pick, some you cannot,
Flavious sees the cruel path of Brackens lost plot.
His fierce link is made, a lightning bolt!
All true Dragons awake to the Keeper's jolt.

The link connects to all parties concerned,
And Bracken sees all he has not yet learned.
The Keeper knows the need for truth spoken to power,
The Keeper respects honesty within those who won't cower.

Hesper meets Flavius in link, and shook to her core,
She first feels the ancient power of true Dragon lore.
Brave Nyber Khan is frozen in place,
It's the first time he's seen Hespers Elven face.

He sees her lost castle of rare purple stone,
Her tragic bed of saffron and lace,
How a cruel changeling spell cursed her to be alone,
And cruelly ripped her from her true sacred space.

His bold heart is smitten with bright elven love,
He glows from within like sun from above.
Hesper's heart sings as she feels it all,
She thanks The Keeper and wonders at his call.

Bracken is caught unawares in this lightning bolt link,
So he shields his mind to try and think.
Inside a deep underground cavern he wisely stays for the day,
Summoning his nine wizards he shows them his way.

Bracken opens his book allowing all nine to link within,
For all nine must go farther than they've ever been.
The Keeper now fly's and the sacred scales are amiss,
Yet greedy Bracken still craves a fine elven girls kiss.

So he commits even stronger for his heart's twisted desire,
And all who stand and oppose him will face magick fire.
Yet the wise Keeper always knows what he needs to do,
Before new time began was the last time that he flew.

So Flavius focuses upon an ancient castle of obsidian stone,
Towards a little blue dragon no longer alone,
Towards mystic battlements of black stone and light,
To help a young wizard survive Bracken's night.

Sweet Hesper has suffered enough hardship and pain,
Flavius will deal with Bracken's unbalanced reign.
The ancient scales will balance no matter the cost,
And these two Elven twin flames will never be lost.

Sweet Hesper deserves her brave wizard true,
The Keeper will do what he knows he must do.
He will fly strong and swift from the center of the earth,
Through golden caverns of crystal towards sunlight and birth.

And the closer he fly's towards sunlight and sky,
The Ancient ones awake and towards the White Dragon fly.
The Rainbow band is coming and they always fly fast,
They speak truth to power and they know truth will last.

For long ago when the earth was sweet- new,
Flew Day Dragons of green, red, orange, and blue,
Alongside their ancient siblings rarely seen in the light,
The Dragons of Day flew with Dragons of Night.

Now the siblings are awakened and fly as one force,
Seeking the Keeper and aligned with sacred, pure source,
Night Dragons of purple, magenta and gold,
Now own the sky with their siblings, all honest and bold.

Disrespect for Gaia is now too commonplace,
So they emerge as a maelstrom, from an ancient, pure space.
They are a sacred mystery and ancient magic in one,
They are aligned with the earth, born from the sun.

They fly boldly from the sacred dreamworld,
A place long their own,
Through the dreamgate into multiverse,
Towards Great Bracken they roam.

For the Keeper now fly's to protect all Gaia's land,
And true Dragons fly with him, a brilliant rainbow band.
The ancient scales are amiss, and they will now be set right,
By a wave of true dragons, a sacred rainbow of light.

The ancient Dragons of the Sea now rise from the waves,
As all the Ice Dragons emerge from artic-cold caves.
The mighty Dragons of the Sun descend from the sky,
The very fabric of the air bends to their cry.

The Dragons of Fire explode from magma white hot,
Leaving smoking volcanoes to mark well their last spot.
Now the Dragons of Desert fly with ancient Dragons of Rock,
For the key has now opened the dream world's mighty lock.

They fly with one purpose for they all come from one source,
The Keeper is now flying, and they all follow his course.
Some choices are made and some are demanded,
An answer to Bracken has now been commanded.

6

General Crokus,
Reconnaissance in Force

Crokus is a general,
A fierce bugbear brave and true.
His thick fur is inky blackness,
His large eyes are steel-grey-blue.

He stands a full seven feet,
In his hobnail boots and leather,
He commands the young wizard's recon force,
Any time, in any weather.

He loves to fly at night on bold griffin back,
Over field, and glen, and darkest hollow,
He commands his troops, elite blood leather scouts,
He leads by example, they always follow.

The wise General has found a flaw
Within Bracken's wicked plan,
A small flaw unseen within Bracken's greed,
May just cost him a bit of land.

For sometimes the smallest detail,
Can carry the heaviest weight.
And many a plan has been laid to fail,
When a commander is blinded by hate.

So Crokus links and things get done,
For this is the warrior way.
The moon is out, there is no sun,
And Shadow warriors love to play.

The scouts form up and griffin link,
Their battle tested formation rules the sky.
They move as one, they never blink,
Blood leather scouts make enemies die.

The bold griffins they fly have blue-black fur,
For twilight and full night is their time about.
Only the strongest griffins and bravest Bugbears,
May become a Blood Leather Scout.

For Bracken has forgotten to consider,
The actual cost of his toxic greed,
And Blood Leather Scouts have a moral code,
Defending Gaia is their ancient creed.

Dark burgundy is the color of their leather,
They are silent on the ground or in air,
They can speak without words, they are invisible at night,
They can take anyone unaware.

General Crokus thinks and link is done,
As a telepathic unit they move and strike as one,
His fearless orders are obeyed as fast as thought,
Greedy Bracken has no idea what he's bought.

For the scouts wear no chain nor armor plate,
And their minds are free of fear and hate,
They have one pure goal and nothing more,
They will bleed Brackens army to its fear driven core.

With black double-edged daggers and the steel loop garrote,
There is no place made a Blood Scout won't go.
Thick battle axes are slung across every broad back,
And all steel scouts carry is the darkest black.

Impervious to any confusion spell,
Blood Scouts can go where even wizards dwell.
They will lose every battle to win this evil war,
And Great Bracken's dark crystal will soon be no more.

For Bracken has built all his cruel tactics,
Upon a lone platform of lust and greed,
To the ancient concept of noble self-sacrifice,
Bracken has chosen to give no heed.

Bracken's army is the largest ever,
His black armored troops are brutal and bold,
He commands the dark magick of violence,
Timeless, malevolent, and cold.

Yet Bugbears are impervious to most spells,
And wild Griffins are born without fear,
So General Crokus and his reconnaissance unit,
Just keep on coming, gaining ground, growing near.

For General Crokus has his own brutal agenda,
A fierce operation he's given much thought,
For now it matters not the immediate victory,
Only how precise each action is fought

His bold plan has three parts,
Each must be flawlessly done,
Thus the Generals noble sacrifice,
Will ensure young Nyber has won.

For Bracken's army has its eyes,
On the ground and in the air,
And Brackens crystal is not every day used,
Nor his secret underground lair.

And all true leaders of great forces,
Must delegate every day,
Within this leadership strength hides a subtle weakness,
And General Crokus has found victories way.

For Great Bracken's eyes, like Nyber's eyes,
See each the same magic way.
Through the eyes of brave scouts each decides,
Their new plotting, every night and day.

The General's finest commando unit,
Boasts ninety-nine Scouts, well equipped,
And Bracken's arrogant forward observers,
Have no idea they are already whipped.

A general first strikes the eyes, second the food,
Thus Bracken's army might just lose the mood,
For it becomes harder to fight when hungry and blind,
The Generals core tactics can be so unkind.

Step number three,
Of the General's reconnaissance in force,
Will hopefully alter the final battle,
Hopefully change Bracken's course.

For Bracken's precious crystal is a glossy black,
And bold Crokus knows he just has the knack,
To raid in from behind and save the day,
To force greedy Bracken to again parley.

Each Blood Scout knows his mission,
For they have all trained with a warriors glee,
The Scouts move to position and silently divide,
Into swift groups of deadly three.

Brackens scouts are all heavy armored goblins,
Upon steel plated griffins they proudly ride,
They believe Great Bracken is invincible,
They are swollen with a gluttonous pride.

So three swift shadows at a time,
Blood Scouts pounce vicious on one,
Bracken's slow moving armored recon,
Has nowhere to run.

Two black axes are used on the fierce griffins head,
Thus telepathic thoughts cannot be read.
The steel loop garrote chokes another proud goblin out,
Thus Bracken loses more eyesight and knows not the route,

That Bold Crokus is carving through a wicked dark night,
For a wise General is needed to set things aright.
Outnumbered is not outmatched, tactics will test,
And as a tactical master, General Crokus is best.

Thus it went through a cold, obsidian night,
As General Crokus led well his last magnificent fight,
And when no black armored scouts rode the cold night air,
To dark midnight ground went this brave Bugbear.

One third of his lost force he ordered to ground,
To kill all enemy scouts and every last goblin hound.
He saluted Colonel Balfour, "You must last until dawn!"
General Crokus waved a bloody battle axe and was silently gone.

Thus Colonel Balfour began his hit and run night,
Of the steel loop garrote and the axe thudded fight.
All sentries were silenced with a black, double edged blade,
Then like the kinfolk of darkness, the Scouts would all fade.

Cruel double-edged daggers bled the cold ground red,
As the steel loop garrote silenced screaming dead.
Hit and move, move and hit,
Misty spirits of the night gave ground commanders a fit.

Their rider-less griffins struck from cold black air,
Slashing and tearing with concentration and care,
They enjoyed dropping boulders, invisible from so high,
Thus black armored goblins were crushed from the sky.

The fierce Blood leather Scouts under Balfour's command,
Kept creeping deeper and deeper into goblin held land.
Outnumbered fifty to one, hunted fierce through the night.
Nyber's best and his bravest made their suicide fight.

They spoke truth to power, and they would not bend,
For a message of truth is sometimes hard to send,
Yet they sent it strong and they made it a wall,
"To allow slavery for one, will allow slavery for all."

This cruelty is a path they will never walk,
And now is not the time for talk.
Action is needed once you speak truth to power,
For the new fertile ground will grow freedom's flower.

The proud goblin commanders thought these Scouts
    would soon run,
Yet Balfour refused to break contact, he was a General's son.
This was a fight to the death, doomed Balfour knew it was so,
For his father Crokus had two giant steps still to go.

Dozens of invaders felt black steel that night,
For each Blood Leather Scout that fell in the fight.
The longer they lasted, the better the chance,
That Bracken would fall to Nyber's brave lance.

Step number two of this desperate plan.
Is a swift strike most bold from the rear,
It's a young captain's mission to destroy an army's food,
Reserve weapons and all extra gear.

Yet that is not all this bold captain must do,
He must bait the black dragon this night.
He must make him fly, he must provoke his rage,
To use his weapon of flame in the fight.

For Bracken's luxurious supply line,
Is coiled snakelike in a tight circle behind,
His bold army of goblins and orcs,
And assorted, black armored kind.

So the next brave third of the Generals recon force,
Urged their battle-mad griffins on a suicide course.
The supply line was lightly guarded for no fool would dare,
Venture this close to Bracken's forward most lair.

Yet with flaming arrows and torches bright,
Wild Blood Scouts burned Bracken's supplies that night.
A young captain named Kell led well his last raid.
His fight baited a trap most carefully laid.

They bravely landed amidst the raging, hungry fire,
Waving their battle axes, tempting the ire,
Of the stunned goblin officers commanding the rear,
Not believing their eyes nor what they could hear.

They order their troops to surround the Blood leather Scouts,
And no mercy will be given as they close escape routes.
Yet Kell's Scouts do not flee, they dig in and fight hard,
Their heroics will be sung by many a bard.

For brave Kell's last mission is no hit and run fight,
He must anger great Bracken and goad him to flight.
So it finally begins, Bracken's greedy, cruel night,
With hungry fire, thirsty axe, and a hopeless Blood leather fight.

Be careful what you ask for, you may just get it one day,
Bracken has pushed all sane limits into a suicide fray.
Bracken had to try and own Hesper, imposing his greedy will,
Now Bracken must pay Nyber an expensive wizard's bill.

For power never sees it coming,
When it imposes the one cruel way,
Until the spark of truth ignites right action,
And illuminates a brand-new day.

A good commander must ensure resupply,
This fact alone will make Bracken fly,
The angry goblins and orcs attack in great force,
Yet the Blood Leather Scouts will not stray from their course,

The bold course laid by Crokus, a desperate, hard plan,
Kell's Scouts must hold out for as long as they can.
The fierce link is strong and Crokus does know,
Through Kell's wild eyes how the lost battle does go.

Upon battlements of black stone and light,
Young Nyber holds well a spider web link,
Channeling power to Crokus, Balfour, and Kell,
Helping his warriors fight well and think.

Bracken's troops are fierce in black chain with iron mace,
Beating shields they stream from every dark place.
But for each Blood Leather Scout downed another steps up,
And many goblins drink deep from deaths bitter cup.

Many Scouts are wounded yet just continue to fight,
Swinging gory axes while bleeding through a suicide night.
And Scout griffins dive swift from a cold night sky,
Many a bold goblin archer is cruelly ripped and will die.

Yet these goblin commanders are fierce fighters too,
They tell their brave archers just what to do,
The goblin leaders stand vicious amidst fire in the night,
Urging their angry archers to make a strong fight.

They wait, seething, until Scout griffins dive low,
Then cruel red tufted, black arrows are released and let go.
Four bladed razor tips spin wicked through the night,
Biting deep into Scout griffins as they dive to the fight.

Yet battle-mad griffins are immune to pain,
And countless goblin arrows must fall like black rain,
To strike even one griffin from the bloody night sky,
Many arrows must strike deep for a bold griffin to die.

It's a cruel suicide fight keeping goblin archers at bay,
And the battle mad griffins make everyone pay.
They slash and tear, splattering blood, slinging gore,
Though wounded and pierced deep they come back for more.

Thus rank after rank of proud black armor and bow,
Are smashed by scout griffins, refusing to go.
Dozens of fierce archers bleed and feed the cold ground,
For each brave scout griffin the hungry arrows bring down.

Brave Captain Kell is now covered in black goblin blood,
He fights thigh deep in dead goblins lying cold in black mud.
Still he maintains his link to his strong general's mind,
While threatened by flames in front and behind.

His double-edged battle axe he swings in both bloody hands,
Butchering a bold path through the black armored bands.
The hungry flames are intense, sometimes he is burned,
Yet he throws himself into battle, his own death he has
    spurned.

He sweats hard with the cruel strain of his focus and flow,
Yet stays centered within so the link will still go.
Slashing and spinning, crushing goblins to ground,
A whirlwind of fury, he's freedoms warrior unbound.

For Kell wears no chain nor armor plate,
His clear mind is free of fear and hate,
He has one pure goal and nothing more,
He will face dragon flame and hear the black dragon roar.

Burning wagons provide distraction for Kell's last
    standing fight,
Countless black armored goblins fall dismembered this
    night,
Yet the black tide keeps swarming on, an endless dark horde,
They just keep paying Kell, across a wise general's chess
    board.

Bracken roars long when he catches this link,
He explodes from his lair much too angry to think.
He climbs the blood red sky, above every cloud,
And vents a purple-red flame, deafening loud.

His arrogant mind is not free of fear and hate,
He sees the flames and takes a young captains bait.
His toxic rage inside he lets gather and grow,
It builds him a new fire and he wants to let go.

He dives hard to the battle, to the lost scouts below,
And bares glistening fangs preparing his blow.
He smiles a slave masters smile and sharpens his course,
These warriors will soon feel the full measure of his force.

As a young captain looks skyward, well focused is he,
For this final fierce vision his bold general must see.
He baits well his trap with an axe wave salute,
Bracken catches this calm move, it's at Kell he will shoot.

The remaining scouts protect Kell as he locks the dragon's
    molten eyes,
Their bloody axes keep cutting deep amidst goblin battle
    cries.
The bloody remnant circles their young captain, battle
    frenzied they fight,
Amidst the lost screams of the dead, through a blood river
    night.

The young captain has been bloodied, cut deep to the bone,
Though wounded and torn he stands not alone.
Disciplined focus and flow he keeps strong within,
Maintaining fierce link with his battle commander and kin.

The angry goblins grow frenzied, breaking ranks they cut
    loose,
They have placed their own heads within a general's tight
    noose.
The well-disciplined captain will never break from the stare,
Of Bracken's red diamond eyes and their volcanic glare.

He calmly leaps to the top of goblin bodies piled high,
And locks death link with Bracken, alone in the sky.
He smiles a reckless, fine smile only a young warrior
    would dare,
At the Black Death exploding out of cold night air.

The very first and last battle this young captain ever fought,
A young knight on a chessboard, bravely cornered and
    caught.
This was a fight to the death, a fight for what's right,
Kell's personal fight for freedom will bring injustice to light.

And when the harshest dragon fire of bright purple and red,
Exploded like many suns above his head,
Within the very last instant of the brave captain's young life,
Kell the peaceful warrior, grinned at Bracken's new strife.

For truth to power is always the way,
To bring in the freedom of a brand-new day.
Truth to power is the temple where courage lives,
The more it is spoken the more freedom it gives.

Crokus wept from his ambush sight,
He had lost a third of his scouts and a young nephew this night,
His warrior tears were swift, then truth to power came back,
For he must gain Bracken's crystal, a glossy black.

How the dragon roared his fiery hate,
When he realized the trap and too late the bait.
He had killed those scouts, that much was true,
He had done exactly as he had intended too.

"Make him think he does as he wants to do"
"Let him fight our fight on his path untrue."
Bracken caught a general's final order with a captain's final link,
Their discipline gave Bracken some pause to think.

He had lost the rest of the link when Kell had died,
"I should have captured them!" to the clouds he cried.
For not only had brave scouts died this cold night,
Within the fiery cruel death born of Bracken's mad flight.

Bracken's entire rear guard had perished as well,
Within his own hellish furnace his ugly rage could not quell.
His entire supply line had vanished from the ground,
Every horse, every wagon, every grey goblin hound.

Dragon-fire had melted what a brave Captain had begun,
Burning and charring with the heat of the sun.
Resupply for Bracken is now a thing of the past,
Time is now a question of how long he can last.

A well planted seed can grow a mighty tree,
A deep seed of doubt is now Kell's legacy.
Self-doubt is always the start of any real defeat,
And Bracken began to wonder just who else would he meet?

Every General needs to see,
The most powerful weapon of their enemy.
And Bracken, he had not held back,
When enraged, he spewed his fire attack.

And now General Crokus and Wizard Nyber,
Through the eyes of a most disciplined scout,
Learned much about Bracken's weapon of flame,
His temperament and what he's about.

They learned well his pattern of final attack,
They now know the point where he cannot hold back.
They know a cruel siege is coming and knowledge is increased,
Now the castle will be better prepared for this beast.

Within Kell's sacrifice Colonel Balfour gained a small break,
For Bracken issued new orders as cold as a snake.
"Every Blood Leather Scout serving Nyber's command,"
"Must be captured and placed inside my hand,"

"An amusing and lengthy interrogation I will conduct tonight,"
"This reconnaissance in force has become quite the fight."
"Full frontal assault, every troop in command!"
"Your new objective tonight is Nyber's dear forest land!"

Bracken roared this most loud so any spies might hear,
He summoned his nine wizard generals and gathered
    them near.
"I want Nyber captured, contained, avoid killing at all cost."
"I wish him tortured in front of Hesper, all her hopes
    crushed and lost."

"Now move as a wave and be double quick!"
"This bold move by Nyber is but a cute trick!"
"The night is ours, in the darkness we rule,"
"For the ancient magick of evil is my finest tool."

Every fierce goblin trooper wears a black leather pack,
With three days rations across a broad, hairy back.
For Kell has cost Bracken time's sweet luxury,
Now sweet Hesper must be won as quick as can be.

One of the simplest mistakes that can cost a command,
Is a too hasty decision made in a strange land.
Bracken's first hasty decision he made quick today,
And Crokus smiles wide, with blood Bracken will pay.

Bracken's castle and lands are many day's flight away,
He now must defeat Nyber by tomorrows new day.
He must find new supplies before three days slip past,
For an army without food cannot hope to last.

He assumes to raid Nyber and take all his food stores,
Then return Hesper to his lands and prepare for more wars.
Bracken's black armored forces move as a wave,
Save some hand-picked commandos guarding his most
     secret cave.

The surviving Blood Leather scouts under Colonel Balfours
     command,
Are grabbed by their griffins and plucked from the land.
Thus finally airborne again they fought long through the night,
The fierce goblins they face seem numberless in flight.

Within bloody moonlight above an icy cloud line,
Wrapped in empty silence and numbing cold,
They were flying wheels within bloody wheels,
As a cruel airborne battle did unfold.

They had no fog to make use of,
Only a wide purple sky and glittering starlight,
Yet a dozen wounded scouts,
Kept fighting a hopeless, wicked fight.

They became wild berserkers through the night,
Striving with all they had to make satin dawn,
They combined bloody, black steel,
With hopeless daring and warrior brawn.

They knew well their delaying action,
Has only a suicide end,
Yet from a beloved Generals' tough plan,
The Blood leather scouts will not bend.

So swarmed and engulfed by an endless black tide,
They choose a hopeless fight in cold air, die hard with
    scout pride.
And in a moonlit, velvet sky many goblins soon die,
Embracing cold black steel, hearing a scout battle cry.

Young Nyber launched each good counter attack,
From well-planned positions his troops bravely fought back.
Yet only two thirds of his forces are engaged in this fray,
He saves the toughest third for the castle, for bitter siege
    the next day.

Bracken's murderous forces press close in and tight,
And Nyber fights vicious, outnumbered, a hopeless
    suicide fight.
Yet pressed hard and engulfed, Brackens army all about,
Nyber's blue armored troops chose to stand and not route.

Now step three of the plan, General Crokus does grin,
He will take this black dragon to a place he's never been,
He will teach him new tactics, the commando way,
When he raids in from behind, and he wrecks Bracken's day.

Crokus orders "Dismount" from all griffins,
They are sent to strike the main force from the rear,
Crokus keeps strong link with his best Colonel,
An only son he loves most dear.

His heart broke with the final order,
The one he had to honestly give,
His best soldier would die this night.
So that many more soldiers might live.

From his final point of engagement,
He ponders a dragon's rear lair.
The goblin troops perform guard duty,
With some precision and care.

Yet strong Bugbears are such a stealthy race,
Much more silent than mist or fog.
They creep unearthly silent from their ambush site,
Behind rock, emerald fern, mossy log.

The steel loop garrote takes out some guards,
Thirsty double-edged daggers drink silent some more,
Before Bracken's hand-picked commandos fully react,
General Crokus has stomped through an oak door.

Seven Dire wolves calmly await them,
Countless vampire bats over six feet long.
Yet the bold scouts attack, keeping battle formation,
Singing the Blood leather song.

Any scratch or bite from Bracken's evil pets,
Holds a cruel poison, deadly and swift.
Yet tough leather on the Blood Leather Scouts,
Will help many avoid Bracken's gift.

Orcs stream, screaming from many dark hallways,
As angry goblins climb up from deep underground.
Yet the general's Scouts just keep fighting, unbending,
For Bracken's dark crystal must soon be found.

Great Bracken knew the absolute second,
His charmed, oak door was kicked in and smashed.
He whirled, cursing in darkened rage,
His Commander of guards will soon be lashed.

And Brave Colonel Balfour has been quite busy,
Following to the harshest letter his father's bold plan.
He has finally seen the first rose blush of dawn,
Creeping across a burned and tortured land.

Though his cold body bleeds, his spirit is light,
And the gentle song of Arora stirs his blood.
The black steel of his axe was well fed last night,
And many invaders now feed the black mud.

The disciplined Colonel has been stalking Bracken,
The last scout alive to survive a blood moon night.
He has seen the black dragon curse and whirl,
And speed angry from the supply line fight.

Balfour rides a fierce griffin named Cybele
She is fearless in the cold, red sky,
So they plunge as one towards a dragon's scaly back,
And let loose the Blood Leather cry,

In normal troops this cry would freeze anyone in their place,
Yet the black dragon spins around, astonishment on his face.
For no one ever dared attack Great Bracken, never just like this,
Engaging with him one on one, just ensures death's final kiss,

Yet Balfour refuses to cut and run,
For he knows truth to power is rarely fun.
One day at a time, one hour, one minute,
The war is here and Balfour is in it.

Balfour knows he cannot kill Bracken,
Those black diamond scales will stop a kill.
But those bat leather wings are something else,
And this brave warrior has the skill.

When an enemy has armor and strength too tough,
It is time for flow, this must be done.
When a mobility kill is the only shot,
Leather wings make target one.

Fierce Cybele claws and bites,
On one of Bracken's leathery wings,
And Balfour leaps from Cybele's strong back,
A battle axe he grimly swings.

This mobility kill is their combat goal,
To delay Great Bracken from his secret hole.
To give a beloved father just a bit more space,
So he can keep searching Bracken's secret place.

The desperate axe swung hard has an aim that is true,
And it's an ugly fight they've bit into.
A torn, gory, hole was made in Bracken's tough wing,
Through which the cold, morning air started to sing,

Brave Cybele was the first to be burned from the sky,
The first to taste flame, feel dragon fire, and die,
And doomed Balfour lost his battle axe swung true,
Yet he clings desperate to the hole his black steel bit through.

His double-edged dagger clears a smooth leather sheath,
And he stabs fierce a black wing, above and beneath.
Great Bracken flames, spins swift, and dives,
And finally burns the very last of two warrior's hard lives.

Above a distant battles din lifts a father's torn cry,
For the general still holds battle link in a cold, red, sky.
He feels his burning son impact the hard, red earth,
His only son, he caressed him at birth.

Crokus runs amok in renewed battle rage,
He kills every dire wolf, many bats, and a mage.
His troops caught his fever and went wild as well,
The killing within Bracken's lair became a nightmarish hell.

When all the killing was finally done,
A grief-stricken General knew he had won.
The cold, dark crystal clutched within a father's strong hand,
Makes him lord for a short while within Bracken's cruel land.

"The true way of the total warrior
Is to choose life while choosing death,"
Crokus hissed soft his final words,
With a warrior's glacial breath.

"A warrior's way many think they know,
Yet it's a way most never see,"
"It's the way true warriors always choose,
And it's the only way for me."

He whispered softly to himself,
His link with Balfour icy cold,
His steel-grey eyes were volcanic fire,
As he stared deep the black crystal bold.

He heard the sound of wind, and leather creaking,
The ragged breathing of warriors brave,
He bore the cost of true freedom and courage,
He knew the power of not being a slave.

The general stood strong amidst the fallen dead,
Of armor black and leather red.
Cut deep many times, bit hard and torn,
He called out to Great Bracken with a voice of scorn.

"Come if you dare Bracken, parley with me,"
"Or your precious crystal will cease to be."
"Let us decide today the cost of your crystal so dear,"
"The true cost of your war, your legacy of fear!"

He then let silence wrap around him tight,
And lonely sadness became his only friend.
He waited calm for the black dragon, his battle axe gripped tight,
From a perfect plan a general won't bend.

Many goblin troops began to assemble,
Outside Bracken's forbidden cave.
They peer fierce through the oak doors wreckage,
With gnashing fangs they snarl and rage.

The Commander of Guards, Captain Sorga,
Chose to fall hard upon her own polished blade,
Dying rather than face,
Any cruel punishment Bracken has made.

Bracken sprays a cold magenta flame,
And clears the mob from his crushed oak door.
He cast's well his dragon-fright spell,
And let's loose a wicked roar.

Yet not one Bugbear is affected,
This strange fact causes Nyber much pause.
He ponders intently with all generals in link,
Together they all know the cause.

Brave Bugbears may go where all wizards dwell,
Their kind is immune to all spells wizard-cast.
Yet real dragon magick is something else again,
Against the magick of dragons they cannot last.

So this Bracken cannot be a real dragon,
And all his magick must be wizard-won.
This fact now changes the balance of power,
And the possibilities within past battles not won.

The bold generals and Nyber debate in link,
This hard-won fact they have all just found.
Whether goblin or elf it matters not,
Any wizard can be driven to ground.

Young Nyber was once considered elven foolish,
By much older wizards considered elven wise.
They all proclaimed, "You have no power over crafty Bugbears!"
"They might give you an evil surprise!"

Yet all wizards are trained to know instincts,
To consider inward promptings too.
Nyber trusts all his noble bugbear generals,
And his brave warriors in armor blue.

Any true dragon would employ some fierce bugbears,
Nyber's inner promptings said it had to be so.
Only an elven mind would have an instinctive fear,
Of where fearless bugbears might go.

All those stuffy old wizards who had ridiculed Nyber,
By Bracken had long ago been crushed.
And young Nyber's troops have fought the only good fight,
Where murderous Bracken has even been touched.

As a shape-shifter Bracken would never have guessed,
He would face any fierce bugbear troops,
Commanding and serving amidst blue armored forces,
Patrolling in concentric, tight loops.

General Crokus ponders this link and smiles deep,
Tactics have shifted and he knows how things go.
Something precious to Bracken will forever be taken,
And General Crokus will make sure it is so.

Bracken thrusts his head through the wrecked oak door,
His ebon fangs glisten blood as he lets loose a roar.
Smoke curls from his nostrils, his ruby eyes burn hellish light,
He stares cold hatred at Crokus, at the carnage of his fight.

And General Crokus just painfully stands,
With twelve grim scouts all in leather, blood red.
He smiles a glacial, fine warrior's smile,
Surrounded by black armored dead.

Great Bracken smiles back with an evil smile,
He links with the General for awhile.
He makes his demands with a face full of scorn,
Yet his demands are the place where resistance is born.

"General, you will now quick return my crystal!"
"And fetch sweet Hesper in a velvet cage."
"Then I may kindly spare your worthless lives,"
"And not subject you to my rage."

"My great army now encircles your foolish wizard,"
"My assault last night killed a third of his force."
"Even without the power of my dark crystal,"
"You have no hope to stay my course!"

"I respect you general, for the fight you bravely gave."
"But it's now time to surrender, don't be a slave!"
"I would make good use of a mercenary general like you!"
"Command in strong armor black, shun that weak armor blue!

Those twisted words lightly tossed by Bracken,
Were cold, and cruel, and wicked done.
Yet General Crokus just smiled in triumph,
For he knows his last battle is now won.

For no true general wants to die with a mission unfinished,
Nor leave earth with a victory undone,
And this raid is personal for Crokus right now,
As he remembers a fine colonel and son.

One should never underestimate a reconnaissance in force,
For well-placed commandos can shape the world's course.
Military craft combined with cunning supreme,
Create new moves on the chess board, moves not as they seem.

"Now we all know you are not a real dragon,"
Bloody Crokus whispers softly from deepest strength.
And he carefully places Bracken's magick crystal,
On a granite slab the perfect axe swing length.

"So I must teach you a lesson, fake dragon,"
"It's something hard, something all real generals know,"
"It's about the true nature of leadership and real power,"
"And how my last battle must go."

"True military power over anything,"
"Boils down finally to just one pure way."
"The ability and willingness to destroy an evil thing,"
"Will many times save the day!"

With that said Crokus swung his hungry battle axe,
Like a wounded father who had just lost a son.
He split the black crystal like a broken heart,
And it imploded like a black hole sun.

Crokus and his lost scouts,
Were sucked into a deep void black,
And sad Nyber knew that no wizard made,
Could ever hope to bring them back.

They were beyond all word connected thought,
All symbols and all sound,
Beyond the void that becomes the void,
Within the velvet darkness forever bound.

They had fought brave to the last and now there were none,
For their prison was now a black hole sun.
Beyond time, fused in space, no beginning, no ending,
Folding and weaving without moving or bending.

And Bracken's secret book bound in midnight blue,
With its rainbow cord all multi-hue,
Also vanished with a battle axe swung true,
Within the dark sun old and also new.

For its prison was also the black hole sun,
From which even a multiverse cannot hope to run.
How Bracken screamed in hopeless rage!
To lose all that hard won magick from such an age.

The mystic book he learned to scribe without needing a pen,
He forgot every word and where they had been.
He had not lost his skill, that much was true,
Yet he lost forever his beloved book of midnight blue.

Finally within this arrogant, ancient, shapeshifter,
A little respect began to sprout and grow.
For within a brave, outnumbered, young wizard,
Great Bracken faced a worthy new foe.

For General Crokus and his hard, military lesson,
Beyond death still continues to teach.
Planting Bracken with countless seeds of doubt,
About a precious soul he thinks he must reach.

So the young wizard Nyber Khan,
Looks sadly down from his lofty perch,
His silver tears fall from grey elven eyes,
Riding cold wind towards pine and birch.

He works the very oldest spells of silence,
Sadness, loss, and respect.
He does honor to all the Blood leather scouts,
His lost warriors most elect.

And Great Bracken has not yet realized.
Free will is what it's all about.
All serve and live within this forest by choice,
Every goblin and blood leather scout.

Nyber chants special honor to General Crokus,
And old warrior, brave and true.
He salutes the void with charmed elven steel,
Shimmering freedom in silvery blue.

For freedom is always worth fighting about,
And the free will to make an individual choice.
For if freedom can be taken from the least of us all,
Then all will lose their individual voice.

Wearing purple robes of ancient power,
And his magick gold embroidered hood,
Nyber works desperate his best protective magick,
The last free wizard who could.

Nyber's magick throws shadows of silver and gold,
He sends forth love, and light, and power.
He works the fabric of sound, a young wizard bold,
He stands tall upon his ebony tower.

He sends it all to a place beyond all light,
To give strength, and hope, and peace.
He makes ready for a war he hoped not to fight,
And he prays for the battle to cease.

7

Bracken's Retreat

Great Bracken labored through the bloody day,
Flying all around the front line fray.
Two bat-leather wings had a rip and a tear,
Courtesy of Cybelle the griffin and Balfour Bugbear.

The sharp gifts they freely gave,
Kept right on sharply giving.
The Black dragon was secretly thankful,
Those two were no longer among the living.

The first war spell Bracken cast was "Paranoia,"
He followed up with "Dragon-fright," and then "Oppression."
General Crokus is not the only warrior,
Who can teach a cold warriors lesson.

And brave Nyber kept casting desperate counter spells,
For each wicked spell that Bracken cast.
And the blue armored troops bravely resisted,
Most bitterly, till the very last.

Nyber's six remaining Bugbear Generals,
Each led their troops brave, hard, and well.
Many of Bracken's toughest warriors,
Were baptized into a new version of hell.

From Nyber's strong hands crackled a golden-red fire,
Many black armored troops became a howling funeral pyre.
Using his wizard weapons of flame, and the fabric of sound,
Nyber cast a brutal flame death to attackers all around.

Each of Nyber's bold griffin riders,
Fought battle wise, crafty, and strong.
Still, the black dragon's well armored, murderous forces,
Controlled the air before the misty morning wore long.

Nyber's free troops faced well the hopeless odds,
Fighting fifty to their one.
Not one blue armored troop ran from battle that day,
A battle they never could have won.

Black arrows and spears rained from the mist filled sky,
Amidst the dragon's wicked fire.
Yet Nyber held on, casting energy spells,
And they faced the black dragon's ire.

With blue banners unfurled, they rallied countless times,
Against Bracken's unstoppable force.
They cost the cruel invaders dear for each stolen inch,
Of Bracken's greedy, selfish, course.

Thus many lost battles were fought,
Throughout the hopeless, bloody day.
And each frenzied, bloody battle,
Became a desperate suicide fray.

For each blue armored troop that bloodied the ground,
A full dozen of Bracken's also went down.
Yet before a blood-red sun centered the hot, noon sky,
The last remnant of Nyber's brave infantry were fighting to die.

They were all finally encircled,
Fully swarmed all about,
Yet Nyber's best and his bravest,
Chose a warriors death, not a rout.

They all held to the last,
Until there were none,
Save the final third held back by Nyber,
For bitter siege had begun.

All around the obsidian castle,
For leagues about,
Lay the blue armored dead,
Who had dared block Bracken's route.

The black armored dead lay entwined with the blue,
Death's cold embrace under hot sun finally joins the two.
Nyber's ancient castle of light and obsidian stone,
Lies encircled now by Bracken's own.

There is only an emerald, mossy moat,
And a single bow-shot length,
Between slavery for sweet Hesper,
And Bracken's twisted strength.

How the red sun shimmered heat,
Upon Bracken's black diamond scales.
His fierce goblin troops beat their shields,
Chanting the ancient goblin tales.

How Bracken stands so very proud,
In the bloody mud, under a vicious hot sun,
Surveying this greedy, mindless victory,
He had so coldly and costly won.

He had lost well over a third of his black armored force,
To a young wizard's tough, blue armored band.
Now the fallen warriors of both deadly sides,
Were bleeding and feeding this land.

Bracken had never won such a dangerous victory,
That had cost him so many tough troops.
A little respect now entered his mind,
For the battle theory of concentric, tight loops.

Bracken had assumed to only fight at night,
Yet here he was facing a full sun day.
His power is lessened when exposed to light,
His true nature on full display.

Nyber's ancient castle is well prepared for siege,
With poison arrows and hot oil as well.
If the first struggle for this free land had been tough,
The fighters taking this free castle would pay hell.

The last surviving Bugbear general,
Was now in command of all siege forces too.
The very oldest and craftiest, his name is Levan,
He'd taught his grandson Crokus a thing or two.

General Levan sent forth his best negotiation team,
Subtly reminding Bracken of focus and flow.
Levan did not ask for mercy, he offered none as well,
He just spoke calmly of how lost battles might go.

Levan simply opened up his steel mind,
Freely offering Bracken an honest, bold link,
This deep confidence within Levan gave the Black Dragon,
A strong reason to pause and think.

Yet an honest link was made and Great Bracken did learn,
Of Levan's suicide planning, how costly siege war might turn.
How the way of a true warrior is the truest of ways,
How every battle fought hard brings freedom to slaves.

Thus Bracken learned more about truth to power,
How one day at a time is the rule,
How ignoring right action is a bad idea,
And how greed breeds an obvious fool.

So Bracken absorbed the offered link,
The true vision inside gave him more pause to think.
He saw the truth of battles fought to the death,
He heard freedom defended in every torn breath.

The cold emerald moat would soon be choked,
With the countless bodies of black armored dead.
They would cross it on bodies and barely get wet,
It's deep, mossy waters swirling blood-red.

The last noble stand of this ancient castle,
Would be a wicked, room by room fight,
Swords and axes clashing level by level,
Throughout the day into a full moon, wicked night.

For the ancient castle was well stocked,
Defended, protected, and tight,
Packed with seething arrows of flame,
Awaiting fierce battle tonight.

Levan had burned all the remaining food,
He knew they would all soon be dead,
So even this final victory by Bracken,
Still leaves his troops empty, angry, unfed.

Yet Bracken still firmly declined,
To release Hesper from his greedy claim,
He ended the détente most abrupt,
With the predictable threat of his dragon flame.

Yet war and détente are really the same thing,
And crafty Levan had won some time,
His general's mind turned many wheels within wheels,
Practicing the warriors art most sublime.

Great Bracken chose to think deep and fly proudly about,
He would survey his fresh conquered land.
Newly fertilized with the precious blood,
Of so many warriors from his hardened band.

The guaranteed victory and outcome,
Did little to lighten his mood.
His warriors would need new supply very shortly,
And he had counted on the castles stocked food.

And there it was! Self-doubt again!
Amidst this costly victory he just had to win!
"One day at a time, they will soon learn my way!"
"They will be dead, I'll win the day!"

Yet brave words did not calm Bracken's cluttered mind,
For truth had been spoken to power.
Bracken had his very first tinge of fear,
As he studied the Castle's dark tower.

Bracken pushed all doubt to the dark recesses of his mind,
He began planning Nyber's torture, cold thoughts unkind.
He took to the sky to think things through,
But all he thought of was armor blue.

And everywhere that day proud Bracken flew,
Black blood dripped from his wing.
And where this blood splashed to the earth,
Grew a most unusual thing.

A black rose sprang up from each blood drop,
That fell to earth that day.
Wondrous in shape and form,
Beautiful in every way.

Its velvet petals have a mirror finish,
Diamond black, deep purple too.
Its many thorns are a glossy magenta,
Guarding a stem of midnight blue.

It has a mystic scent composed of lavender,
With hints of the oldest roses that ever grew.
It will make one forget their life,
And everyone they ever knew.

So if you ever go out on a walk about,
To explore a distant land,
Never pick the beautiful wild black rose,
For you are sure to prick your hand.

For if ever such a rose,
Were to prick a curious hand,
You would fall into endless slumber,
And never leave that land.

So it was, great Bracken proudly flew,
Pondering on this hard fought day.
When suddenly an ancient trumpet blew,
Putting all his warriors at bay.

The bold face of a white dragon appeared,
Filling up the noon-day sky.
"I will be there in one hours' time!"
The Keeper roared from way on high.

"I fly with ten thousand true dragons!"
"Our mighty wings block the sun from the sky!"
"How dare you impersonate our noble form!"
The ground shook with the Keeper's bold cry.

Great Bracken stared angry at the Keeper's face,
He had fought much too hard to lose this race.
"Then today, white dragon I will fight in the shade!"
Yet his words spoke fierce soon started to fade.

That seed of doubt was now growing again,
Despite the smugness of Bracken's grin,
He pondered all he had lost within battles din,
He knew now that death was the true wage of all sin.

Bracken knew his time was now undone,
His war was over, the Keeper had won.
Without his magick or dark crystal, he had no chance,
The Keeper of all Sacred Words was now part of the dance.

How Bracken roared his fiery hate,
His war for sweet Hesper had been waged too late!
He had won every battle yet lost the war!
His ancient crystal and book would be no more.

"A curse on you Nyber! On your land and your lake!"
"For protecting sweet Hesper whom I wished to take!"
"A curse on your forest, every tree and clear brook!"
"And a curse on that Crokus for destroying my book!"

Bracken boiled Nyber's lake and soiled the silver sand,
Then he ordered retreat for his tough, goblin band.
Time had become an enemy, that much was true,
He had lost this contest to warriors in blue.

Bracken thought to himself in darkened rage,
About his first retreat as a dark magick mage.
"Within an hour we will be long gone from here,"
"If we abandon our wounded and all extra gear."

Ten thousand dragons no wizard could beat,
Thus Bracken accepted his first bitter defeat.
His tough goblin generals heard new orders that day,
"Retreat back to our lands, tolerate no delay!"

For if war is détente more intense,
And détente is war less intense,
Bracken knew it was now time to leave,
And pull back to his side of the fence.

So Great Bracken shifted into the shape of a crow,
His ancient magick inside he let gather and grow,
He called up black fog for furlongs about,
Hiding his doomed army's retreat, covering their route.

As a crow he flew to his ruined forward lair,
And found his secret red crystal of which none were aware.
A scrying adept, he conjured his favorite room,
And he was back in his secret castle, just a half hour past noon.

He flew swift from his castle and hid deep in his wood.
He gathered his pet crows about him as any dark wizard would.
He knew his lost army was three hard days away,
He would hide out as a crow for many a day.

He must stay deep within his flock and not link as well,
If he hoped to avoid a real dragon's hunting spell.
Bracken was now prepared to lose all he had wrought,
Yet he would not lose his skills, nor all abilities they bought.

Great Bracken would build his dark sorcery again,
Greater, stronger than it ever was before.
He may have lost this battle for sweet Hesper today,
But he had just begun to craft a better war.

Though he cannot at this time use his magick,
Nor in any way aid his lost army's cruel plight,
Their noble diversion will help him avoid The Keeper,
And all the Rainbow Dragons might.

For everything in life is secretly a lesson,
Defeat and victory too.
And Bracken has learned the lesson of a lifetime,
Taught by warriors in armor blue.

His total victory was only a bow shot away,
Yet the Keeper had flown and seized the day.
If Flavious is involved Bracken knew he'd crossed a line,
He will wait out the carnage, allowing old scales to re-align.

For the Multiverse never errs,
All true wizards know this is so,
Bracken will elude the Keeper's mighty grasp,
For he has many places he still wants to go.

Crokus has taught Bracken the true definition of power,
And The Keeper now flies the sky.
The Dragons of Light will ensure that true peace does flower,
As The Dragons of Night ensure enemies will die.

Flavious has demonstrated the strength of right action,
Bracken now understands how high he must go.
If he wants to defeat a mighty Keeper,
He must become a much deadlier foe.

Sweet Hesper will one day be his,
If it's The Keeper of Sacred Words he must fight.
Great Bracken will just grow and re-group,
For the right time when all timing is right.

Nyber and Crokus, that accursed general,
Have taught Bracken well, concerning focus and flow.
Bracken learned a hard lesson about the true nature of power,
And how the best laid plans sometimes go.

Any remnants of his lost, defeated army,
Strong enough to survive the next few days,
He will carefully nurture back to a cadre strength,
And teach them even more deadly ways.

He will consider the use of mercenary Bugbears,
To train and bolster his new army throughout.
For he now has a desire for a new kind of soldier,
To train up a new kind of scout.

And once this arrogant Keeper has done his terrible worst,
And finally returns to keeping his dusty old words,
Great Bracken will assume his favorite Dragon form,
And cease to fly anymore with the birds.

8

The Arrival of Flavious

Ancient Dragons flew and filled the sky,
Bouncing light from the sun, way on high.
Ten thousand colors filled the turquoise air,
Around the Keeper now freed from his crystal lair.

The colors of day with the colors of night,
Painted the sky with their magical flight.
Blended together they became a rainbow of one,
Great Bracken's forces are now undone.

The sacred trumpet blast heard from way on high,
Only once before shook the earth and sky,
Only once before rippled all the waters of earth,
On the very first day of terrestrial birth.

And on the final day of our Sun and our Earth,
The same trumpet will sound to signal rebirth.
Its sacred vibrations are felt in each soul every time it is blown,
Its Seven Angels are mysterious, it's true player unknown.

As Flavious descends from the sky his emerald eyes are
    pure sadness,
For the root of anger is fear, and he is not filled with
    madness,
The ancient Scales are unbalanced, and this causes him pause,
He has long considered the nobility of Nyber's brave cause.

Flavious see's black fog for furlongs about,
Hiding Bracken's trail, a murderer's route.
The Keeper's cleansing spell makes the fog go away,
A proud army is exposed to the Dragons this day.

The fierce Dragons of Night dive swift on this force,
Of black armored warriors on death's final course.
These ancient dragons of colors only seen during night,
Bring horrid weapons of flame to fight their favorite fight.

Yet the lost goblins display no fright,
Their steel flashing purple and burgundy-blood red.
They look skyward towards fierce dragon light,
They know they will fight until dead.

Led well by Bracken's nine best wizards,
They face the mighty dragons of night,
But it has all become a hopeless fool's errand,
For their victory is now lost forever from sight

They make their first charge on wild griffin-back,
With ancient battle cries, sharp lances, and sword.
Yet they never complete their fatal charge,
Engulfed by flame from a wild dragon horde.

Bright glowing gasses and flame,
Explode hot from the sky.
A searing, multicolor incineration,
Is the way most die.

Yet some griffins keep flying,
Trailing orange fire as they soar,
They crash, burning onto tough dragon scales,
And they die with a last, earthly roar.

Flavious makes link, a lightning bolt,
All dragons feel the Keeper's jolt.
"Hunt them to the last, may only the strongest survive!"
"Capture this Bracken, I want the imposter alive!"

So the Grim Reaper's bloody Scythe,
Drank a full harvest that day.
Through the one sided battle,
Through the hopeless, cruel fray.

Eight of Bracken's nine wizards,
Were burned to the ground.
The fallen troops lay in twisted piles,
Wrapped in a brutal absence of sound.

The screaming dragon-fire became a dancing death,
Led by ancient spells upon dragon breath.
The Dragons of Night know their purpose well,
As they make every battle a nightmarish hell.

Yet the lost wizards led well their doomed army,
They managed to make some dragons pay,
For every dark wizard burned vicious from his mount,
And crushed to cold earth that bloody day.

Nine Dragons of night were finally forced to the ground,
Swarmed by hundreds of burning griffins, finally downed,
Then hundreds of goblin ground troops, with battle axes
    and sword,
Hacked them and slashed them like a frenzied, doomed
    horde.

Yet those downed dragons still struck,
With flaming clouds of bright gas,
Melting black armor to skin,
In a horrible mass.

Bright dragon scales and obsidian armor,
Became a hideous, flaming mound,
Mystic fires of purple and red,
Were seen miles from cold, muddy ground.

Yet Bracken's last dark wizard, Ceres,
Fought a desperate fight, long, hard, and well.
And she managed to save herself and her infantry,
By the clever use of a simple spell.

A spell so old and easy,
She almost let it slip completely away,
She almost forgot the first rule of sorcery,
That the simplest spell might save the day.

Her wild magick inside she let gather and grow,
With an ancient changeling spell she mastered long ago.
As Bracken's young apprentice it was her favorite trick,
To escape from her chores and work not a lick.

Ceres was only a small child when she learned this one well,
Her mystical, magical, smoke changing spell.
Upon reciting this spell from the recesses of her mind,
Her fair body did change and begin to unwind,

Ceres became smoke and she drifted away,
Along with all of her infantry on this terrible day.
She decided to stay as smoke for at least a week,
Thus she and her infantry would be harder to seek.

Yet her fierce griffins were immune to fear,
They would not stop fighting the night dragons so near,
Her griffins would not listen, they refused to retreat,
They chose death in a false battle, and so chose defeat.

They all fought griffin vicious to the vicious last,
And they all met death in a fiery blast.
They all embraced the Grim Reaper while still in the air,
And not one made it back to Bracken's dark lair.

When the Dragons of Night finished scorching the ground,
There were no goblins, no griffins, nor a grey goblin hound.
They could account for eight dark wizards, but crafty
    Ceres got away,
With three hundred goblin infantry, on this bright,
    bloody day.

Flavious sighed deep as he surveyed about,
His perfect emerald eyes never needed a scout,
Flashing from within a thousand shades of green,
Glowing with sadness and wisdom, intense, never mean.

The scales of Gaia were now balanced, he felt this as well,
It seems that Bracken will live in spite of this hell.
To unbalance the ancient scales is the greatest of sin,
So Flavious centered himself and focused deep within.

His ancient magick inside he let gather and grow,
He went to a dark place few earth wizards could go.
A place in the multiverse that takes, rarely gives,
A place of cold secrecy where hopelessness lives.

A new black hole sun, a prison bleak,
A noble General Crokus the mighty Keeper did seek.
No earth wizard made could have brought them back,
Yet Flavious, First Dragon, was born with the knack.

For the Old Ones who fly multiverse, universe is not tough,
And the Keeper of Sacred words has all the right stuff.
Within a supernova of gold light a noble deed was quick done,
General Crokus stood brave under a hot, burgundy sun.

And thirteen scout bugbears clad in tough leather, blood red,
Stood in silence, blinking hard at the numberless dead.
All were bloody and wounded, black axes held tight,
Hardly believing they had survived the wicked, black night.

Stunned into silence by the awful truth within war,
Praying like soldiers for peace, lasting peace evermore.
For truth to power has been spoken, the coin exchanged to
    be free,
One day at a time has now turned freedom's key.

Crokus never even blinked,
Anyone sane might have though he would,
He called out to Flavious in a voice strong and calm,
As only a sad father could.

"Noble Keeper you know this is not right!"
"I ordered my son to a brave death in an unfair fight!"
"To allow slavery for one allows slavery for all!"
"My son did his duty and answered the call!"

Crokus spoke his heartbroken words, cruel, sad, and true,
Thus Flavious had one more spell left to do.
One great spell never attempted before,
By Dragon Magic from a sacred core.

The Keeper addressed the General with great respect,
"Crokus, you are a warrior, most elect."
"Your brave son was a warrior to his golden core,"
"Death is a path chosen by warriors whenever there is war."

"I will attempt this thing you ask of me,"
"If Gaia's scales stay balanced then it will be!"
"Free will is the law, the essence of Source,"
"If the scales stay balanced you may sometimes change course."

With an explosion of turquoise and royal blue light,
The Keeper's deed was nobly done.
Where once general Crokus so sadly stood,
Now stood Colonel Balfour, his only son.

Upon tall battlements of black stone and light,
Young Nyber wept openly at this wondrous sight.
For yet a second time he had lost his old friend,
His tears became quicksilver riding icy wind.

Flavious summoned the mighty Dragons of Day,
And focused them on a mystical way.
They flew all over the tortured, burned, blackened land,
A wondrous, healing, rainbow band.

Using the most ancient spells of healing, love, and light,
They carefully repaired the damage from Bracken's cruel fight.
Red poppies now bloomed where they had once been burned,
A turquoise lake gently rippled, though once boiled and churned.

Countless fish of silver, red, orange, and blue,
Leap and swim in this lake again made new.
The magic forest of pine, emerald fern, and ancient stone,
Is again green, deep, and lush, and it all smells new grown.

The bear and boar, wood fairies and gnomes,
Live again undisturbed within safe woodland homes.
When the Dragons of Day finished their sacred task,
In new growth and peace all the living did bask.

The Dragons of Night made funeral pyres of the dead,
Collecting all armor and weapons of dread.
Grinning with the wild eyes of those loving to fight,
They stocked well the castles armory on that full moon night.

Mighty Flavious kept chanting the old poems of rebirth,
With respect to Gaia's scales and the plan for green earth.
For now the struggle was done and the healing must start,
For all good decisions are made in the mind and the heart.

The Keeper's tears fell from emerald eyes,
Falling swift to a brand new earth,
And where each tear touched the ground,
A precious emerald found brand new birth.

And when all the healing that could be, was finally all done,
Nyber understood the true price of the freedom now won.
Night was riding in thick, the bloody day was all gone,
And the magick forest was safe for the doe and the fawn.

The mighty Keeper now rose in the coolness of night,
His diamond scales scattered silver in the full moon light.
"Our work here is done, we will now be away!"
"Please feel free to link with me any fine day!"

So the Dragons of Day with the Dragons of Night,
Flew with bold Flavious in a magnificent flight,
Between earth and moon, radiance beyond light,
The ancient forces of peace with the ancient forces of might.

Not since long ago when the earth was still new,
Had flown day dragons of green, red, orange, and blue,
With war dragons whose colors are not seen in the light.
The mighty Dragons of Day with deadly Dragons of Night.

Night Dragons of royal purple, magenta and gold,
Those mighty Dragons of Sunset, fierce, honest, and bold.
How the harvest moon's golden light bounced from those scales!
The harmonic sound of their singing is like killer whales.

Young Nyber and Hesper and all warriors still sound,
Kept their eyes bathed in this light, their feet on the ground.
Taking in colors most never again see in the night,
The mystic frequency band of multifaceted light.

No Aurora Borealis was ever as bright,
As this swift legion of rainbows on a full moon night.
Not one warrior moved until they saw the magic colors no more,
Not one eye was dry at the end of this war.

So the victorious wizard, Nyber Khan,
Gazes for hours from his lofty perch,
Loving, feeling, and cherishing,
An ancient forest of pine and birch.

He will never hunt humans for sport again,
He seeks to harm no living thing,
For young Nyber has seen The Keeper fly,
And he's heard all the dragons sing.

He has learned the secret of one day at a time,
He knows how to speak truth to power,
He knows all true battles start and end within,
He sends spells of transformation from his tower.

9

The Rescue of Calibus

Calibus smelled flames from a distant fight,
Heard dragon fire and explosions of light.
Though far away he heard Death's final cry,
He felt griffins and goblins burned from the sky.

Calibus caught the battle links from many warriors
    cast wide,
Thus he learned the status of battle for each bloody side.
When he was caught within the emerald light of the
    Keeper's mighty link,
He learned many things within a swift eye-blink.

He saw an ancient purple castle, of intricate, elven
    worked stone,
An old place lonely Hesper as a princess called home.
A special place long lost where she once had been,
A space long denied her due to Bracken's cruel sin.

He learned of a cold, magick jar wrapped in a silver cord,
Tied to an ancient, gnarled, oak tree.
And how, if one found this secret oak and broke this jar,
Princess Hesper could once again stand free.

He endured black fog, intense flame and heat,
For the iron chain in granite rock he could not beat.
He endured no food, and no cool water near,
Yet his Griffin spirit stayed strong in the absence of fear.

Dehydrated now, starved near to death,
He called aloud with his last breath.
And from a simple farmhouse near,
A little girl his call did hear.

She slipped swift from a warm bed of cotton and down,
As she lived far from any town.
A cherry wood dresser she opened wide,
And grabbing her clothes she stretched and sighed.

A farm girl she was, and brave, and true,
She wondered aloud about that strange call and who,
Or what might have called it? In the dark of night?
She dressed quick, for a country girl needs no light.

She ran fast from her farm, and her dear father's home,
Alone in midnight blackness she dared to roam.
A strange creature was hurt, from its call she could tell,
She filled a bucket with sweet water from her dear father's well.

The moon was full, the night was good,
She snuggled deeper within her hood.
She crossed a meadow of red clover and oat,
Thankful for the leather and wool of her coat.

Suddenly to her surprise,
Wondrous colors lit up the skies.
A blaze of unknown colors lit up the moon,
Ending for her much too soon.

In the warm afterglow of blue star and sky,
A magnificent white dragon flew close by,
His diamond scales were white, yet multihued,
Prism like, no light subdued.

Reflecting brighter than sun on polished abalone shell,
His diamond-crystal scales showed all colors well.
He smiled at her a dazzling, handsome smile,
And he bid her keep searching for a while.

In a flash of emerald light he flew far away,
Her fear was banished and kept at bay.
She turned and ran swift to a dark oak wood,
And she prayed that she might do some good.

She found brave Calibus on this moon filled night,
She gave him cool water and she suffered no fright.
And lo and behold! What a wonderful thing!
Without moving his lips, she heard Calibus sing!

A wondrous poem filled with longing and verse,
All about handsome Nyber the wizard, and sweet Hesper's curse.
She was deeply moved when he told her his name,
She feared from his wounds he was crippled and lame.

She left him the water and ran swift back home,
For there were now a few places she just had to roam.
She ran quickly to her father's forbidden iron forge,
On the way she picked apples for Calibus to gorge.

She was told the forge was dangerous, to never touch it's tools,
But Tara decided to test those rules.
For her father taught her to always do what is right,
To not fear the darkness and to spread the light.

So she took a steel hammer, a steel chisel too,
And ran swift back to Calibus to help him cut through,
The horrid, cruel chain attached to that rock,
And using hammer and chisel his freedom unlock.

It took half the night, yet the tiny girl would not quit,
Even though her eyes were heavy, little Tara still hit.
The fierce Griffins eyes glistened as she struck the cold stone,
This brave human child, unafraid and alone.

"I'm seven years old tomorrow, Tara is my name!"
"I'll gladly help you walk, you seem so hurt and lame."
"You can come to our house! And stay forever there!"
You will get better really quick under fathers gentle care."

And bold Calibus right then decided,
As he watched her strike that chain,
That this child was now his lifelong friend,
And he shook his golden mane.

Finally the cold iron chain was split asunder,
And bold Calibus then stood free.
Calibus and Tara stared each in wide eyed wonder,
Under the spreading branches of an old oak tree.

Calibus tried gamely to use his wide wings,
But he was broken, clawed deep and torn.
Little Tara rubbed his gold-black fur,
And she pondered most forlorn.

"My dear father will just have to be,"
"Understanding of the way things are."
"Come on Calibus, do the best you can,"
"Our warm barn is not very far."

The human child helped him as best she could,
Through those dark woods and across a long field.
She knew her barn had warm straw and oats,
She would warm him and get him healed.

Calibus hobbled, sometimes he crawled,
Yet not once did he ever quit,
He made Tara's warm barn with the rosy dawn,
He gave the two horses quite a fit.

Yet little Tara calmed those two horses,
As she made Calibus a warm straw bed.
She ran to the kitchen for black bread and cheese,
And she picked more apples, a luscious red.

So Calibus was fed, and made warm and dry,
He stretched out in the straw with a contented sigh.
Purring and preening like a gigantic, golden winged cat,
His pain began to lessen, and he liked where he was at.

Tara fetched him a wool blanket from her own cedar chest,
And a down pillow from her own little bed.
She snuggled up in the warn straw next to huge Calibus,
And they ate apples, some cheese, and black bread.

And big Calibus, he started gently snoring,
Before little Tara was even near done.
Yet soon after sweet Tara finished eating,
She slept also, in the warm morning sun.

Little Tara's father got quite a surprise,
As he did all his chores at first sunrise.
Yet he was wise and very well read,
So he knew it was a griffin in that warm straw bed.

There was his precious Tara, just as snug as could be,
Safe and warm for all to see.
He took out the nervous horses to let them graze,
Wondering at the strangeness of these last few days.

Last night he had dreamed a most wonderful dream,
He saw dragons fly and he heard them all sing.
He had met a white dragon who had calmed all his fear,
Who had let James know that a wild griffin was near.

This same white dragon that left in emerald green light,
Had left peace in James's soul, and a calm, restful night.
So James waited patiently as Tara slept warm and snug,
He sipped peppermint tea from a handmade mug.

The gentle arms of Morpheus released Calibus first,
The Griffin looked for more water to quench his great thirst.
Calibus then saw James yet he felt no alarm,
For there was kindness in those eyes, and peace grew at
      this farm.

Calibus made link and to his great surprise,
Recognition flashed deep within the human's grey eyes.
"These humans can accept a link!"
This fact gave Calibus some pause to think.

"We are not really that different, you and I,"
Thought James in link with a wink of his eye.
"My name is James and you are most welcome here,"
"You've gained some nasty wounds I fear."

"I am an excellent healer though,"
"And I would like to help you before you go."
With that said James smiled, turned, and strode away,
To gather herbs and ponder sacred magick this day.

Now brave Calibus knew many things have changed,
To hate and fear all humans was most deranged.
For all hatred is made when cruelty is done,
And ugly deeds can be done by most anyone.

For the deeds of bugbears, griffins, goblins, or elves,
Can be cruel or kind or in between.
Good or evil is a path chosen within ourselves.
A way of life can be both kind and mean.

An old way of life that no longer serves universal good,
Can be invalidated by new growth, once understood
All beings have the potential for evil, and potential for good,
A long ancient fact now newly understood.

Tara and James have endured loss and strife,
Yet they have chosen a path of good this life.
If these humans have done so, then others have too,
Calibus understands what he must soon do.

He must heal fast and to Nyber fly swift,
He must speak of human kindness and Tara's fine gift,
Of freedom and help from the cruel chain and hard stone,
Because of Tara and her father he did not die alone.

There must be no more callous hunting of humans,
In the heat of day nor starry night.
Just because they were born human,
No longer makes it right.

For no one picks their culture,
Their parents or their kin.
And for those things no one should be hated,
Being born different is not a sin.

Of this new understanding young Nyber must know,
And Calibus the brave griffin, will relay it just so.
For we are all children, born of the sacred fire of All One,
And peace has a destiny where war cannot run.

James was soon back with herbs that help sustain life,
He took in a sharp breath at the fierce griffins' strife.
One wing was clearly broken, the other deep torn,
He wondered how the griffin had lasted till morn.

James used his tools in a most clever way,
And removed the rest of the chain with the collar that day.
Calibus was so cruelly torn from stern to stem,
James wondered what beast could have tackled him.

He cleaned the many wounds and bandaged Calibus tight,
And Tara fed Calibus right well, morning till night.
They braced strong the griffin's wing, his mighty foreleg as well,
James wondered from what great height he had fell.

In three weeks' time under their fine care,
Calibus took his first, short flight in cool air.
His thick griffin fur of black flecked gold,
Was all shiny now and his nose was cold.

In three more weeks he was even better still,
He could sprint the long meadow and run the hill,
In three more weeks he was strong and quite sound,
But he made excuses just to stay around.

First Tara, then James, and Tara's little brother too,
Learned to ride Calibus above clouds in the deepest sky blue.
"You are welcome to stay," James often said,
And beneath thick fur the griffins face turned red.

Calibus was ashamed to admit to these new friends most dear,
That human kind he once hunted due to ignorance and fear.
That he used to hunt humans, night or day,
That human kind were once his most favorite prey.

He knows one thing in his heart most crystal clear,
No goblin nor wizard had better ever raid here.
Nor in any way cause these kind people harm,
Nor bring any destruction upon this fine farm.

For Calibus is now determined to well protect,
These new friends he holds most dear,
For he is a born warrior, deadly and fierce,
And he knows well how to banish all fear.

Yet the sad time of parting has come much too swift,
And brave Calibus was thankful for this family's fine gift,
Of friendship and kindness, and dandelion wine,
Of Tara's sweet singing, how her small face would shine.

When he was finally able to say goodbye,
All their eyes glistened with diamond tears.
He made a solemn griffin promise to soon return,
And he calmed their saddened fears.

He told them all of Hesper's plight,
Of the young wizards war, of Bracken's cruel fight.
How Hesper's sweet form was captured within a silver jar,
And how he hoped his young wizard might get that far.

Then James told Calibus of a darkened wood,
Filled with fern and rock, where giant oaks still stood.
Where only the bold Watchers ever dare to roam,
Yet not even brave Watchers would call that place home.

For a wild Harpy now lives in this darkened wood,
Making an unhappy home amidst fern and serpentine rock.
She unwillingly guards an ancient tree and jar,
With a cruel riddle none could hope to unlock.

She can fly on wings of bat leather black,
She has sharp talons in place of each hand.
A feathery serpents tail coils around her smooth form,
She was cursed deep within Bracken's dark land.

She sings in a fine voice as sweet and clear as a bell,
Within the classic line of her face there is mythic beauty
    as well.
Her hair is the magick color of fairy spun gold,
Her full woman's body is most tempting and bold.

Her flawless skin is the color of polished Tan Oak,
Her almond shaped eyes glow burgundy, like all ancient,
    fairy folk.
She moves with a strong grace, her sad beauty twisted
    supreme,
And she glows with a strange light, a dark angel's sunbeam.

Only a few Watchers have ever met her, or spoke with her long,
They have sang her the old poems and heard her sad song.
For she was once a fair maiden of a strange beauty blessed,
But she had refused Bracken's advances, and his marriage
    request.

And like Hesper she was changed into a magical beast,
Her anguish became dark energy upon which Bracken
    does feast.
Now she lives enslaved to a curse only the dead ever heard,
Her new form is part maiden, part fearsome beast-bird.

Yet if one guesses her riddle the sad Harpy is free,
She gains back her life and who she used to be,
And she will be free to return to her home by the sea,
For this hopeless, cruel riddle is her freedom's lost key.

The tree is free, the jar is free,
To whoever unlocks her clever verse,
And she is free forever more,
From Bracken's wicked curse.

Yet it is only a few Watchers who know well of her place,
Of the Harpy's sad song, or her beautiful face.
The path to Dark Oak has been hidden quite long,
Only the Watchers have kept the way hidden in song.

"Watchers?" Calibus purred most distressed,
"I thought they were only an ancient myth!"
"No one believes that Watchers are real!"
"At least no one I've ever spoke with."

"The Watchers are quite real!" said James with a grin,
"We've met and spoke, they are human kin!"
"If anyone can help you gain that silver jar,"
"The ancient Watchers can, for they have been that far!"

"From snowcapped peaks, barren of trees,"
"To redwood ridgelines in ocean breeze,"
"Shadow is the place these ancient Watchers dare roam,"
"Big fir and fern tip grace their home."

"Watchers they are called,
Old Ones, or Dark Ones too,"
"Nocturnal, they run secret caverns deep,
Calling out to me and you."

"Secrecy is their game,
Yet they like some to know they are here,"
"The occasional tuft of red-brown fur,
Will mark a passage near."

"Sometimes mud will steal a footprint,"
"A twilight hiker will catch a green eye glint,"
"And backpackers, unafraid to go remote,"
"Might hear an old poem from a Watchers throat."

"In the day they sleep far beneath the land,"
"At night they hunt, a far roving band."
"Cascading streams are the trails they walk,"
"Fast water hides the sound of the Watcher's talk."

"Stalactite caverns enormous underground,"
"Coat the ancient bones of their dead, forever unfound."
"Thus stalagmite cocoons their headstones become,"
"Hiding the red ocher and flowers brought by some."

"Their green eyes gather starlight and make night as day,"
"The evening stars are their suns and light well their way."
"They know many secret valleys and hidden rifts,"
"They know thermal streams and nature's gifts."

"An occasional lost Watcher will stray too long in the light,"
"How the humans then fuss and take such a fright!"
"Yet all Watchers are wise to the fear based, human way,"
"So they keep the soft night, and let their new cousins have day."

"Sometimes my ancient cousins will visit my farm,"
"They gather apples at dusk and cause nobody harm."
"I look forward to their visits, we talk long through the night,"
"Yet the Watchers always leave before dawn shows her light."

James smiled sadly as he spoke those words,
He knew the Watchers were as elusive as rare wondrous birds.
"You fly swift to Nyber, let him know you are alright,"
"I'll try to call out the Watchers, there is a dark moon tonight."

Calibus gave his thanks, nuzzled hugs all around,
Then his powerful wings took him far from the ground.
He flew back towards a castle of obsidian stone,
Back to Nyber and Hesper, no longer alone.

He would tell of these humans who have kindness and love,
How they live lives of peace and know the songs of the dove.
How they seek understanding, kindness, and light,
How they attempt cooperation before attempting a fight.

For young Nyber must now hear of these things,
And learn of the bounty that peace always brings.
He must learn the secret grace of which right action sings,
For when truth speaks to power freedom has wings.

So under a waning moon of glowing topaz,
As stars of rubied Safire lit a velvet sky,
From his place of silence and secrecy,
James sang forth an ancient cry.

An ancient poem created before language was made,
James whispered it loose from deep within,
It traveled the hills, and vales, and caves,
To the places only Watchers have been.

In a secret language beyond word connected thought,
Known well by newborns and the innocent too,
The vibration traveled through water and air,
And into the land of warriors in blue.

James then settled in to wait out the night,
And seek the old ones who have long shunned the light.
To talk of Nyber and Hesper, brave Calibus too,
He was seeking wise counsel, for their council is true.

The first Watcher to arrive was bold Serviel,
A crafty Pathfinder for the oldest clan, Daden.
They spoke long of the curse, the cord, and the jar,
And a blue dragon who was once an elf maiden.

Serviel agreed to call council,
And speak with the Old Ones this night,
All his elders know well of Bracken's dark lands,
And they know well of his latest, cruel fight.

Serviel and James grip the wrist,
They nod in silence and thus agreement is spoken.
Respect thus earned in right action,
Means the curses of Bracken are broken.

If his elders say it will be done,
Then all clans will hunt this wicked jar.
The big Pathfinder turns and begins a tough run,
For tonight Serviel must travel far.

James again raises his calming voice,
Climbing the cool, magenta sky.
And once again travels an ancient poem,
Riding an ancient cry.

The mystic cry of all true Watchers,
An Elders blessing riding a star filled night.
A blessing and greeting for all who can hear,
And who dare work at doing what's right.

10

The Transformation of Hesper

The young wizard Nyber Khan,
Kept right on hunting day and night,
To find that wicked silver jar,
And ease sweet Hesper's plight.

He cast his strongest spells of seeking,
And he prayed they would come back swift.
He sorely missed his wild griffin, Calibus,
Whose strong friendship had been such a gift.

He loosed his magick hood from around his head,
Letting flow his hair of silvery-red.
His steel-grey eyes glowed hopeful, warm, and kind,
As he formed seeking spells with his wizard mind.

His well-muscled arms and strong elven hands,
Rest on sword belt and hilt, as he surveys the lands.
His thoughts were golden eagles that soared on cold wind,
Speeding with intention all the magick he could send.

So the forest elf, Nyber Khan, looks down from his lofty perch,
Cherishing a bold new forest, fresh scented with pine and birch.
Atop battlements of black stone and light.
His elven heart is warmed by the peaceful sight.

When he caught an old familiar link in the flame colored sky,
His head snapped towards a setting sun,
For a wild griffin flew like a burnished gold streak in the sky,
And Nyber knew well this noble one.

"Calibus is home!" Nyber shouted,
And he laughed aloud as Hesper gained the link.
She was turquoise flame as she flew the sky,
Before the young wizard could even blink.

She flew all around brave Calibus,
And her fine laughter led him straight home.
She bombed him with questions about where he had been,
Before his strong claws could even claw black stone.

Nyber hugged hard his wild griffin friend,
And he laughed that this this might be so,
For he had thought this wild griffin free,
Was dead many a dark day ago.

And Calibus told them everything,
All about little Tara and her father as well.
How he owed them his life, how they ended his strife,
How Tara saved him from Bracken's cruel hell.

And young Nyber told Calibus the brave griffin,
About never wanting to harm anything.
About the Dragons of Day and the Dragons of Night,
And the magic harmonics when they start to sing.

They spoke long of the Watchers and a silver jar,
Nyber Khan swore to break that riddle afar.
They would find this tragic Harpy of the dark oak wood,
Though the risk was great, somehow, they would.

The cord of mystic, silvery hue,
Will be unraveled from the ancient oak tree.
The cruel spell on the harpy will vanish too,
And Princess Hesper will finally be free.

Nyber linked with his newest general, Balfour,
"You must link with the Watchers tonight,"
"They are stealthy, silent, and strong,"
"Break contact if it looks like a fight."

Nyber linked with his oldest general, Levan,
"You must search the four directions many ways."
This almost emptied the garrison of troopers,
For the searching will consume many days.

And Dragon Hesper, she flew above silky clouds,
Her diamond scales glistened shades of silvery blue.
Brave Calibus and Nyber flew swift beside her,
And Nyber's personal bodyguards too.

Glad they were that another hunt had begun,
For all of them none too soon.
The golden light of the sun was their guide by day,
At night, the bronze light of the moon.

Nyber's personal guards wore armor blue,
Their spears and round shields tufted burgundy red,
Horned helms of polished silver spouting golden plumes,
Graced every tough bodyguards head.

They flew on young griffins of golden fur,
Swift as the wind these bold ones were.
They scan sky and ground with an eagle's eye,
As strong wings pump and griffins purr.

The night passed long, the day passed soon,
Yet still they rode hard a cold, clear sky.
Sleeping not until the second day at high noon,
For wild griffins just love to fly.

Within the summit of a glacier topped mountain,
Lie secret caverns hidden by white velvet snow.
Inside of these caverns the crafty watchers were meeting,
Speaking of a riddle they all wanted to know.

Each clan had an elder present,
They all spoke without words in the dark.
They spoke long about a jar and where a sad harpy sang,
And how Bracken could leave such a cruel mark.

A bugbear force now patrolled their lands,
Attempting link many times in the night.
The Watchers would chuckle as they hid from them well.
Yet they loved watching the wild griffins in flight.

To link with the bugbears was out of the question,
They gleefully avoided General Balfour's every attempt.
For their silence and secrecy springs from an ancient
    tradition of safety,
Yet this Bracken they all hold in contempt.

The most respected elder, Satrina,
The very wisest and most profound.
Has decided to assist these two future life partners,
And she gathers the strong clans all around.

Yes, she will help this blue dragon Hesper,
And this young upstart wizard Nyber Khan.
For she respects how he fought a desperate battle for
    freedom.
And his will to protect the doe and the faun.

For Satrina understands the high art of discernment,
She always listens to the whisperings of her heart.
She will speak Pathfinder truth to power,
In this conflict she will play her part.

She summons her best pathfinder Serviel,
He kneels focused to absorb every word.
Satrina sings the ancient poem that tells of Dark Oak,
And summons with Serviel a cunning, strange bird.

A giant stellar jay with feathers of purple and blue,
And a bold crown of feathers purple and black.
Satrina's riddling bird, her most beloved pet,
And Serviel had better just bring him safe back.

She extends her warm hand to strong Serviel,
And he kisses the All Clan signet ring.
A promise to accomplish well his secret mission,
And take good care of this bird he must bring.

He stands swift and bows with respect,
He begins a pathfinders sure footed run this dark night.
On his broad shoulder is perched the riddling bird,
And he hopes this strange bird will not bite.

He used many secret underground caverns,
On his approach to Bracken's Dark Oak.
Soon Serviel and that clever riddling bird,
Became quick friends and started to joke.

Satrina's bird taught Serviel some clever limericks,
And some were quite naughty too,
Thus Serviel started to really like,
This strange bird all purple and blue.

Within secret caverns underground,
Where fairy light rainbows still abound,
Serviel runs and learns the riddling sound,
While Bracken is weak, he will invade his ground.

When they finally emerged from deep underground,
The cavern opened near a great waterfall.
The moan of leaves in wind twined with water sound,
Birthing Serviel's pathfinder call.

From a secret mountain top to an ancient oak valley below,
There is no place made a pathfinder can't go.
With light or without, it matters not,
There is nothing hidden that Watchers can't spot.

A golden haloed moon of lapis lazuli,
Held hostage a perfect, stygian sky.
So pure and beautiful that the riddling bird,
Stopped chattering and let out a sigh.

Beneath a rugged, gnarled oak, ancient and tall,
Stands the harpy sentry, fierce and strong.
She stares long at Serviel by the old waterfall,
And she motions him to be long gone.

A thousand meter stare arcs between the two,
Harpy sentry and a Pathfinder bold.
Serviel's eyes flash emeralds, the stellar jays are Safire blue,
And the Harpy's are just sad, and glacial cold.

Perched within the branches of the oak is the silver jar,
Wrapped in a wondrous, silver cord.
Serviel spies it's reflection from the opposing shore,
And the valley stream he calmly starts to ford.

"Pathfinder stop!" The harpy's voice is ancient song,
"Near this dark oak you do not belong!"
"This is a space only for me and never you!"
"You walk your walk on a path untrue!."

Her almond eyes became glowing rubies that lit up the night,
A wondrous beauty and horror, Serviel gasped at the sight.
He had heard the poems and the tales, but still he felt fear,
Yet he was a Pathfinder first, and his mission was clear.

Yet the strange bird whispered calm into Serviel's ear,
A strange little magick song.
"Tell her she is the one made unnatural here,"
"At Dark Oak she does not belong."

So brave Serviel spoke as the bird did advise,
And silver tears welled up in the harpy's sad eyes.
She sighed a musical sigh and stared a thousand miles away,
How Serviel felt, no words could say.

"Ask for her riddle, by the Gods you are slow!"
"I just may tell Satrina you know!"
So brave Serviel did ask as the bird did advise,
And even greater sadness welled up in her deep ruby eyes.

The harpy bowed her head then shook it twice,
When she looked at Serviel again, her face was not nice.
"Tell me this Pathfinder most bold!"
"How can one winnow the gravel from gold?"

"What word is a tool for grading sizes of rock?"
"Yet forms a smooth question for the mind to unlock?"
"How can you cut the lightest chaff from the grain?"
"What is used in some harvests but never in rain?"

"What means spreading throughout, describing many a flaw?"
"What word roots from harvest, yet describes errors in law?"
"You have only a swift moment to answer me well,"
"Or your brave life is forfeit at the sound of my bell."

In a sharp talon she held a golden bell to the sky.
And she released yet again, a sad, musical sigh.
She looked hopeless, fierce, and beautiful, all in one,
Serviel just knew he was now undone.

"Well, have you anything useful or clever to say!?"
Said that loud bird on his shoulder in a shocked sort of way.
"This pitiful riddle is not even worth the name!"
"As a conundrum it's fairly weak and lame!"

"Go on now Serviel, speak well to this lovely beast!"
"Just give her the simple word she is seeking at least!"
The stellar jay chuckled loud and whispered just one word,
And Serviel could not believe this rude bird.

The bird whispered loudly some more; it could not be true!
Yet brave Serviel answered as the bird instructed him to.
"Riddle is the answer to this riddle you seek!"
Serviel sweated and waited for the fine harpy to speak.

She smiled a gentle, fine smile and put down her golden bell.
And Serviel grinned mighty big, for all was now well.
"Right you are foolish pathfinder dear!"
And she winked a pretty eye at the stellar jay by his ear.

Her serpent wings, tail, and talons all vanished as well.
Of a prettier woman, they both never heard tell.
The old poems said she was a beauty and it was all true,
The riddling bird was deep smitten and to the Harpy he flew.

The jay sang his sweetest to the pretty woman,
With a warm gleam of joy in his eye,
He told her of noble bugbears,
Searching for Dark Oak close by.

"We will build a bonfire for those bugbears,"
"They will find and rescue you soon!"
"I am truly sorry we cannot stay awhile,"
"But we race tonight with the moon!"

"Boy are you slow!" sang the bird to Serviel,
"And I'm telling Satrina too!"
"If it was not for me knowing riddles,"
"This fine harpy would have eaten you!"

"Well I am a Pathfinder," said Serviel most clear,
"I have strength, endurance, and I control fear."
"I may have been eaten, and I may have not,"
"I did however, find this spot."

The dark spells of Bracken have no more power here,
There is a fine purity in Serviel's strength.
So he ignores the noisy bird as he grips well the cord,
And unravels swift it's knotted, silken length.

In moonlight, liquid gold, he holds aloft the silver jar,
His large hand turns it this way and that,
His emerald eyes widen, catching light from distant stars,
And Serviel purrs like a giant, auburn cat.

Serviel chuckles deep as he fords quick the stream,
He vanishes in the swift waterfall.
He's well covered his tracks near the fording site,
And he sings now his oldest call.

For none may know a Watcher was about,
And he sings his oldest song.
He seeks the stalactite caverns deep underground,
Where he and the ancient fairy folk belong.

Before the jealous, golden moon fled the ebon sky,
He reported to his elders with a soft watcher's sigh.
Satrina the Elder accepted her bird and the jar,
Then she summoned the strongest pathfinders from all
    clan's afar.

"Travel with bold Serviel, and guard him from harm,"
"You will all leave this evil jar at Kinkind's farm!"
Satrina winked at Serviel's mischievous grin,
As her stellar jay whispered in her ear about all that had been.

So to sweet Tara's farm they all traveled swift,
To leave the silver jar, the Watcher's fine gift.
When morning arose, they kept to the shade,
But come cool nightfall again, the farm they made.

At the edge of the farm they sent forth the cry,
And James answered them back with an old poem and a sigh.
Thus Pathfinder Serviel finally delivered the jar,
With the blessing of Satrina and the Old Ones afar.

Left by the well of James and little Tara's farm,
The magical jar was safe and free from harm.
Stealthy Serviel sang the goodbye song,
And began again his run, for the night was long.

And James, he sang the ancient kinship poem,
As he sang his ancient cousin safely home.
Then he turned swift, running to his farmhouse near,
And he called aloud to his children most precious- dear.

"Just look at what our cousins have brought!"
"The cruel jar within which her true form is caught!"
Then James, his sons, and little Tara too,
Gathered together under a sky of midnight blue.

Their magick within they let gather and grow,
They built up a link they had never let go.
They all centered together to call Calibus swift,
Casting wide a swift link that sang of the gift.

The gift from The Watchers who are silent and strong,
A gift for sweet Hesper who had suffered so long.
And Brave Calibus how his soul sang deep within,
When he caught the fine link from The Watcher's kin.

To know that James now held the silver jar,
To know that Nyber and Calibus would fly that far.
To know Hesper will gain back her elven form,
Win the longing of her heart and be elven norm.

Nyber and Hesper had diamond tears in their eyes,
As they flew towards that farmhouse swift,
Brave Nyber began the ancient spell of opening,
To prepare for the Watchers kind gift.

They all flew swift under a moon of rare bronze and gold,
Their spears and shields reflecting moonlight bold.
They rode the ancient sky of burning Safire stars,
With not one billowy cloud to behold.

How Nyber pondered upon the strangeness of days,
And thought long and hard of all the ways,
That he was blessed and lucky too,
To love the land, sweet Hesper, and armor blue.

It seemed their long flight might never end,
Yet through a hidden valley at a wide river's bend,
They found a quiet farm with well cared land,
To a soft field of purple clover descended the band.

And that is how James, his sons, and little Tara too,
First met fierce warriors in Armor blue.
And they met other griffins with golden fur,
As they rubbed Calibus's neck and made him purr.

Food was procured and they made a moonlight feast,
As many warriors flew in from the distant east.
A wild link was sent out; "Let the Gathering begin!"
"Let all feast together as creations kin!"

To finish the Spell of Opening would require the day,
And Nyber was thankful he had found his way,
To this hidden farm managed by kind humans and kin,
To know he had made right choices from deep within.

The breaking of the jar must be under full sun,
Thus Bracken's evil spell will run.
So they all reveled together long through the night,
And awaited the dawn to set things aright.

At the first misty glimpse of Arora's' silvery-pink glow,
The well prepared Spell of Opening was released and let go.
All formed a circle around Hesper at first morning light,
As young Nyber urged that spell into flight.

The silver jar was cracked with a thunder bolt!
All warriors felt the magic jolt.
The very fabric of the air wavered in heat,
As the evil magic of Bracken began its retreat.

Another flash of turquoise and the jar shivered and shook,
It grew so bright, it was quite painful to look.
The jar melted and sizzled, it was finally absorbed by the
    ground,
Where a blue dragon once stood, now none could be found.

A wondrous elf maiden stood in her place,
Beautiful of form! So lovely of face!
Her elven tresses held the colors of spun rubies and gold,
Her almond shaped eyes were luminescent, sea-green,
    and bold.

Clothed only with the sun she shone well in that place,
Her skin was pure satin, her lashes pure lace.
Nyber came forward and wrapped her in his cloak,
And they all welcomed her finally back into freedoms folk.

Nyber held Hesper, and alone in a seething throng,
They embraced tight in the sun, elven long.
Many cheers went up as warriors beat their shields,
And there was laughing and dancing throughout Tara's fields.

They all had so much fun at this first Gathering,
James proposed one for each and every year.
Once a year a harvest moon gathering,
Little Tara grinned from ear to ear.

Now Nyber knelt on bended knee,
"Sweet Hesper please be wed to me,"
When Hesper smiled her eyes were emerald sun.
As she took the strong hand of her chosen one.

She sang, "I'll gladly wed you wizard dear!"
"Now stand up quick and hug me near!"
"Hold me close and kiss me long!"
"And our home is the place I will always belong!"

So Nyber answered swift her sweet request,
And he did his very wizard best.
He caressed her back, gently pressed her near,
He cherished her slow elven heartbeat, warm and dear.

When his lips found hers, a lightning bolt!
Each lover felt the other jolt.
They kissed each other long and well,
Thus even deeper into sweet love they fell.

A huge cheer went up amidst the crowd,
From wild griffins and warriors, deafening loud.
When the kiss was done each gazed long and deep.
And promised each other's soul to keep.

Then suddenly a strange sound was heard,
It descended slowly from way on high,
At first a soft tone, like a lone temple bell,
Graced everyone from a turquoise sky.

Then more wondrous tones within that lone tone,
Were heard and felt by all below.
Then harmonic tones within those tones,
Like countless temple bells did grow.

Then suddenly the very sun was blocked!
As countless dragons filled the sky.
Becoming one glittering rainbow of all colors bright,
The fierce dragons flew close by!

All stared in silence and wonder,
As the dragons sang their ancient song.
As colors within colors and warm tones within tones,
Whirled and swirled the horizon long.

Thus mighty Flavius Pontificus Calendula,
The ancient Keeper of all Sacred Word,
Landed with the Dragons of Night and Day,
For of a fine gathering he had well heard.

His diamond scales now glittered a multi-hue,
As glowing crystal magic may sometimes do.
The Dragons of Night with the Dragons of Day.
Conjured ancient spells of blessing the lovers' way.

"We have brought you a gift and a guest in one!"
"You will never guess where we have all been!"
The Keepers cat like eyes were brilliant green,
And they flashed mischief along with his grin.

"Do not mistake me now regarding Balfour,"
"For he is a fine new General, brave and true!"
"But we thought you have long missed some others,"
"Whose eyes are steel-grey-blue!"

With that said the Keeper laid back his wings,
And twelve mighty wings they were,
And from the center of the Keeper's broad, scaly back,
Leaped two shadows of inky, black fur.

General Crokus and Captain Kell stood tall before them,
In hobnail boots and leather, blood red,
They wore polished sharp steel inside harness and sheath,
For they are both fine warriors, well bred.

Nyber and Hesper ran to them,
As Balfour raced through the surging crowd.
They mobbed them as one and hugged them tight,
And the wild cheering became most loud.

"It is so good to be The Keeper,"
Flavious stated calm with a devious grin.
"Sometimes you are able to do those things,"
"That you know just should have been!"

So the bright Dragons of day hosted a huge wedding feast,
And well toasted the new couple most bright,
Then the wildest reception ever thrown,
Was well hosted by those wild Dragons of Night.

So if you ever venture out on a walk about,
To explore some distant land,
Feel free to smell those bright poppies red,
Swim the turquoise lake with the silver sand.

And should you ever come upon an ancient castle,
Carved of the blackest obsidian stone,
Approach the crystal gargoyles and come on in,
You don't have to be afraid nor alone.

Young Nyber is so much kinder now,
Because he fears no living thing.
For he has seen the mighty Keeper fly the sky,
And heard the fiercest dragons sing.

And that young wizard Nyber Khan,
Still peers down from his lofty perch,
With loving self-protection,
On a magic forest of pine and birch.

Upon ancient battlements of black stone and light,
With Princess Hesper he proudly stands,
And weaves brand new spells of love and light,
That he learned from ancient rainbow bands.

The dragons come to visit from time to time,
To spin their ancient tales.
The Watchers listen and do not speak,
For they hear no battle wails.

The bucks are bold, the does are safe,
Many fawns now grace the field.
The trees are lush, the fish are swift,
The land is fully healed.

For this was the place where truth first spoke to power,
This is the place where freedom was won.
And now this is the place where the black rose flower,
Can no longer hurt anyone.

For peace has come and now it grows,
The time for life is here.
For courage came and now it stays,
Because brave warriors faced their fear.